"A CARDASS_____ WARSHIP HAS A_____ BENEATH US," LIEUTENANT DAX SAID.

W9-AVR-661

"And we're being hailed by a Bajoran ship," Major Kira added.

Commander Sisko sighed. "Put them both on screen." The two alien commanders, the Cardassian Gul Danar and Bajor's Captain Litna, appeared before him. "You are both in danger," Sisko told them. "The last ship in this area was torn apart. We are investigating the cause."

"We know the cause," the Cardassian commander said. "Bajoran terrorists . . ."

"You're the one attacking our planet, Gul Danar," Captain Litna said.

"No one is attacking anyone else," Sisko said. "Go home. Get your scientists busy. We need to solve this quickly or it will destroy all of us."

"Stop protecting the Bajorans, Commander," Gul Danar said. "This is the last time they will terrorize us. We will defend ourselves. If another of our ships is attacked, we *will* begin a counterattack on Bajor."

"That is a declaration of war!" Captain Litna shouted.

"That is a declaration of intent," Gul Danar said quietly.

Look for STAR TREK Fiction from Pocket Books

Star Trek: The Original Series

Star Trek: The Next Generation

Star Trek: Deep Space Nine

For orders other than by individual consumers, Pocket Books grants a discount on the purchase of **10 or more** copies of single titles for special markets or premium use. For further details, please write to the Vice-President of Special Markets, Pocket Books, 1230 Avenue of the Americas, New York, NY 10020.

For information on how individual consumers can place orders, please write to Mail Order Department, Paramount Publishing, 200 Old Tappan Road, Old Tappan, NJ 07675.

STAR TREK®
DEEP SPACE NINE™

THE BIG GAME

SANDY SCHOFIELD

POCKET BOOKS

New York   London   Toronto   Sydney   Tokyo   Singapore

The sale of this book without its cover is unauthorized. If you purchased this book without a cover, you should be aware that it was reported to the publisher as "unsold and destroyed." Neither the author nor the publisher has received payment for the sale of this "stripped book."

This book is a work of fiction. Names, characters, places and incidents are either products of the author's imagination or are used fictitiously. Any resemblance to actual events or locales or persons, living or dead, is entirely coincidental.

 POCKET BOOKS, a division of Simon & Schuster Inc. 1230 Avenue of the Americas, New York, NY 10020

Copyright © 1993 by Paramount Pictures. All Rights Reserved.

 STAR TREK is a Registered Trademark of Paramount Pictures.

This book is published by Pocket Books, a division of Simon & Schuster Inc., under exclusive license from Paramount Pictures.

All rights reserved, including the right to reproduce this book or portions thereof in any form whatsoever. For information address Pocket Books, 1230 Avenue of the Americas, New York, NY 10020

ISBN: 0-671-88030-6

First Pocket Books printing November 1993

10 9 8 7 6 5 4 3 2

POCKET and colophon are registered trademarks of Simon & Schuster Inc.

Printed in the U.S.A.

To Nina
for all those nights of pizza and Trek

THE BIG GAME

CHAPTER
1

THE LIGHTS FLICKERED for the sixth time. The turbolift jolted, stopped for a moment, then kept climbing. Commander Benjamin Sisko breathed a quiet sigh of relief. The last place he wanted to get stuck was the turbolift, and with the odd problems that had plagued the station for the last hour, getting stuck was a distinct possibility.

The flickering lights had him bothered, although not quite enough to give up his lunch with Jake; Sisko and his son rarely had enough time together. They had planned the lunch for days, fasting in the morning, so that they could overindulge in all Jake's favorite foods: spaghetti, Norellian twist bread, chilled Ruthvian salad, and chocolate cake à la Jennifer. They had just gotten to the twist bread when the call came in from Ops. Maybe, if Sisko was lucky, this emergency would only take a few minutes and he would be back in time to eat half the cake himself. He would never admit it aloud, but he had a weakness for chocolate.

The lift stopped at Ops. Sisko stepped out, glancing briefly, as was his custom, at the Cardassian architecture: the almond-shaped portals on the top tier that revealed stars, Bajor, and the docking bays; the multi-level operations area, and the prefect's office—now his—straight across from the turbolift. He had never thought he would feel comfortable here, but during the last few months Ops had become the deck of his own personal starship.

This afternoon the deck was nearly empty. But he could feel the tension, almost as if it had been etched on the walls. He sighed. He had a hunch the chocolate cake would have to wait.

Major Kira Nerys stood behind the operations table, her gaze on the viewing screen. Hands clasped behind her back, feet spread in military precision, she looked all business. Lieutenant Dax sat at the science console, her fingers moving rapidly along its surface. Other than that, Ops was empty.

"What's so important about a Ferengi ship that I had to leave my lunch with Jake?" Sisko asked. He kept his voice low, but neutral. No sense being upset about missing time with his son if there was a true emergency.

"The Ferengi ship seems to be suffering from the same power fluctuations that we are," Dax said. "They requested a docking bay nearly two hours ago, but have made no movement in our direction."

"Power fluctuations?" Sisko said. "You mean, we're having more serious problems than the lights?"

Kira did not look at him. A sign that she probably

should have called him earlier, but did not want to disturb him. He wouldn't mention the lunch again.

"The fluctuations go through all of our systems in a random pattern," she said. "The computer locator is off-line; I have someone searching for O'Brien. The outages aren't serious yet, but I'm afraid they will be."

Sisko walked down the steps toward the operations table. First things first. The outages were important, but Kira already had that under control. The Ferengi ship was the big question. Sisko glanced at the main viewer where the Ferengi ship hung motionless against the blackness of space. If he didn't know better, he would have thought that the ship was crippled. "Open a channel," he said.

Dax moved to do so when the station rocked wildly as if it had been hit by a photon torpedo.

Sisko lost his balance and fell against the operations table, banging his arm and sending shooting pains through his shoulder. Dax slid under the science console, and Kira cried out behind him.

Alarms went off, their blaring cries of warning sending Sisko back to the day his wife had died. For a moment, he lost himself in those flaming corridors, lost himself in the feel of Jennifer's dead body clasped against his breast. He swallowed the memory, hard, refusing to let it overcome him.

He glanced around. Smoke filled Ops.

The lights went out. Blackness overwhelmed him. The acrid scent of smoke dug into his throat. The backup generators kicked in, but the low-level lights only made the smoke more opaque.

"The Ferengi ship is breaking up." Lieutenant Dax's calm, intent voice broke through the pandemonium. She clung to the science console as the station rocked again.

The Ferengi ship was the least of Sisko's worries. All the screens had jumped to life, reporting problems and outages throughout the station. Warning lights blinked all over the operations table. He pulled himself up to it, trying to loosen the pain in his shoulder, wishing he could see better through the smoke haze. The smell of burnt electrical wiring had him worried. "Tractor beam? Can you hold the Ferengi ship together?"

He had to shout over the wail of the alarms.

"Attempting that," Dax's calm voice replied.

Kira had pulled herself to her feet. Out of the corner of his eye he saw her shadowy shape mount the rickety stairs and hurry to the engineering station. Where the hell was O'Brien?

Sparks hissed from loose connections. Sisko crossed to a free console and did a quick run-through of the station's life-support systems.

"A few ships have been knocked off their moorings in docking bays ten and twelve," Kira said. "Reports of jammed doors. Lights down all over the station. No serious damage to the station, and no casualties."

The constant rise and fall of the alarms served as counterpoint to the three officers' staccato conversation. The smoke had grown thicker. Sisko held back a cough.

"Life support is working," he said. The system did not register any sustained hit. No telling what caused the entire station to rattle so.

The main lights came back on, flooding the smoke-filled room with brightness.

"I've got the Ferengi ship," Dax said, "if the tractor beam holds."

He scrambled up the short steps to the science console. Dax had returned to her chair, her rounded figure and bright eyes a testimony to the fact that she was no longer the old man he remembered. But just as competent. Maybe even more so.

According to the readouts, the Ferengi ship was the largest Sisko had ever seen. It seemed to have sustained damage at the same time as the station.

"Kira," Sisko said. "Shut those alarms down and find out where that smoke is coming from."

"Yes, sir," she said.

Dax glanced up at him, her wide, calm gaze helping him focus. The Ferengi ship. The docking bays. The lights. "The tractor beam seems to be holding," she said. "I'll bring them into docking bay. . . ."

"Make sure you stay away from ten and twelve," he said, in case she had missed that bit of information. He twisted to see the main viewer. The Ferengi ship at a glance seemed to be all right, but he knew that only the tractor beam held it together.

Sisko punched the console, moving his attention away from the station's interior functioning. Nothing anywhere near the station except that Ferengi ship. No ship that could have fired a photon torpedo, no record of a cloaked ship appearing at the moment of the shot. Nothing to show that anything had happened, except the damaged Ferengi ship and those damned alarms.

Slowly, Dax eased the ship toward the station.

The lights blinked again, but stayed on. Then, without warning the tractor beam quit.

"What is going on?" Sisko snapped into the smoke-filled air.

"The ship is breaking up," Dax said.

Sisko reached for the board, but Dax's hands flew across it, trying everything he could think of just a moment before he could say it. The board did not respond. The tractor beam was simply gone. Thirty seconds stretched into an eternity.

"It's no good, Benjamin," Dax said. "I've done everything possible to reestablish the beam."

The alarms seemed to have grown louder, more insistent, demanding that something be done. The Ferengi ship appeared to bounce in space as if it were a sailing ship in a rough sea.

He turned to Kira. She was still at O'Brien's station, a frown marring her delicate face. "Get a lock on the crew of that ship and be ready to beam them here."

"Do it quickly," Dax said. Her voice was very low and cold. "The ship won't last much longer."

"Only three on board," Kira yelled out just as the alarms stopped.

Her voice echoed off the walls, demanding and impertinent. It grated on him almost as much as the alarms had. "Then get them out of there."

Her fingers danced over O'Brien's board. On the main view screen the Ferengi ship broke up as if it had been hit by a hammer. Sections of the ship flew in all directions.

Kira was shaking her head. They must have acted too late. Sisko steeled himself.

Then three forms shimmered on the small transporter unit. They were close together and it took a moment for the shapes to separate into two Ferengi and a bald humanoid alien. The center Ferengi was ancient and huddled over. He had huge ears with hair growing out of the centers, and his wizened face looked as if it were about to melt at any moment. The other Ferengi was younger and had ears the size of Sisko's palm—normal for a Ferengi. The younger Ferengi and the humanoid, an Hupyrian servant with pale skin and an overhanging brow, had a firm grasp on the ancient Ferengi who leaned on a staff with a gold-pressed latinum head.

The Ferengi's dark, intent eyes looked directly at Sisko and the Ferengi's mouth turned down into an ugly frown. A shudder of distaste went through Sisko. Zek. Grand Nagus of the Ferengi. The closest the Ferengi had to a ruler.

Sisko sucked in a deep lungful of the smoky Ops air and stood up straight to greet the guests. What was the Nagus doing here? And why?

"Nagus," Sisko said, bowing just slightly to show his respect, a respect that he didn't feel. The Nagus typified all the elements of the Ferengi, good and bad. "I trust you are well from your ordeal?"

"How dare you attack our ship?" The younger Ferengi—Krax, the Nagus's son—let go of Zek and stepped off the platform toward Sisko. "We had no weapons and—"

"We did not attack your ship," Sisko said. He would not get into a fight with the leader of the Ferengi. "We had nothing to gain by doing so." He swept his arm around Ops. The smoke had thinned a little. "And, as you can see, we suffered from the same problem you did."

"Really?" Zek said. "You haven't lost a ship, Commander. A small fortune in gold-pressed latinum was on board." Zek paused to let his words sink in. "Do we share a problem? Have you lost a fortune in gold-pressed latinum?"

Heat rose in Sisko's cheeks. He would have to act quickly on this matter. The Nagus could be lying, and he would try to make the Federation responsible for the money.

"We don't know the extent of damage here yet," Sisko said. "But whatever hit your ship hit the station."

"So you may have lost money," Zek asked as he eased himself down from the platform with the help of the bald humanoid. Sisko didn't let the relief show on his face. As long as the Nagus thought they had the same problem, he would be less likely to blame Starfleet. "Have you located the culprit?"

Sisko glanced over at Dax and she shook her head. "We don't know what caused the disturbance yet," Sisko replied. "But we hope to have some answers soon. Kira, find O'Brien, now."

"Yes, sir," she said.

But before she could even turn back to her panel the lights again flickered and the entire station lost power and went dark.

And the alarm sirens started again.

CHAPTER
2

THE LIGHTS FLICKERED as Quark mixed the last of the drinks and picked up his tray. He glanced up. That had better be the last time the lights even pretended to go dim. Quark needed lights. He needed cool air. He needed everything to be perfect.

The Dabo girl swooped by Quark as she headed into the back room carrying a tray of drinks. Her slender nose was wrinkled and her lips turned down in disgust. Quark grinned and followed her, a tray of drinks perched on his small hand. He had given her the more noxious concoctions: a Hot Foaming Beer Dart, which smelled of fermented cat box, for the Meepod; a Klingon Cordial, made of wortweed and steaming pungent gray smoke; and a Falconian Licorice Slimmer, with baked grub worms (disgusting! they should only be served cold) and imported banana slugs, for the Sligiloid. The tray itself sent off an odor so foul that when Quark took the drinks off the replicator, Rom fled the bar with his hand over his mouth.

Quark carried the more common drinks: saki, for the two humans in the corner; Romulan ale for the Romulans near the door; and Bajoran sipping sherry for the terrorist who had talked his way into the game. Quark slipped through the door just as the Dabo girl ran out, her normally pale skin green and her eyes watering. He paused for a moment to survey the room.

It was set up for the largest Seven Card Hold'Em Poker Tournament ever held in the sector. Quark was not fond of poker. Dabo was his game. But poker brought the true gamblers, the ones willing to risk everything.

Ten tables, each with eight chairs, filled the room, their green felt surfaces beautifully crafted to Quark's exact specifications. He'd been planning this, the quadrant's largest poker game, for years, well before the Federation's takeover of the station. The takeover had delayed his plans for a short time, until he learned that humans—even humans who wore a Starfleet uniform—loved games of chance. Some of the best officers in Starfleet were known throughout the quadrant for their skill at poker. Quark had invited all of them. He had spread the word of the game to each ship that had docked at the station. He had hired, at great expense, professional dealers so that the professional gamblers would think the game was on the up-and-up. And it was, for the most part. No one would know that with the house take and his skimming, he was going to make more gold-pressed latinum than ten Ferengi could carry.

The tournament was due to start the next morning

and today Quark had invited players to enjoy the room and play pickup games, making sure, of course, that the house took its "fair" share. Three games were going on at the back tables. Quark hurried to the first, where most of his drink orders had come from. He set the saki down in front of Harding, a bald human with a well-chewed, unlit Ferengi cigar hanging from his mouth.

Harding pulled his cards close to his chest and picked up the tiny bottle of rice wine. "Hey!" he said to Quark. "It's not hot!"

"You didn't specify hot," Quark said. "And your friend here"—he set the remaining bottle in front of the other human player—"requested his chilled."

Harding took the Ferengi cigar from his mouth and leaned toward his companion. The other man, Klar, was tall for a human and slender, with silver-white hair and cold silver eyes. Harding had spent most of the afternoon talking Quark into letting Klar play. Quark had wanted proof that Klar could play to tournament levels. Klar's entry fee of one hundred bars of gold-pressed latinum, plus an extra 10 percent, had convinced Quark.

Klar picked up his bottle and pulled the tiny cup off the tray. Without saying a word he poured the rice wine into the cup and drank.

Harding grimaced. "You will never learn, will you?" he asked, jabbing his unlit cigar in Klar's direction. "The best tobacco is in Ferengi cigars. You ruin them when you light them, like you did this morning. The best alcohol is Japanese saki—hot saki, so that it goes into your system quicker—"

"I don't want it to go in quick," Klar said. His voice was slow and measured, its tone as cold as his eyes. "I want to remain alert. We're here to play poker, remember?"

"Hard to forget after that little scene this afternoon." The Romulan woman sitting next to them tapped her long, thin fingers against her chips. Her name was Naralak, and she had come alone. Quark set the Romulan ale in front of her. She ignored it and him.

The other players at the table—the tall, thin Irits with its featureless obsidian face, and the round, orange Grabanster with its thick fur and wet-dog smell—pretended to be studying their cards.

"I am the best player in the quadrant," she said, her voice mocking as she quoted what Klar had said when he sat down. " 'You can't have a poker tournament without me.' " Then she laughed. "We have had many tournaments without you, Mr. Klar. And I will wager, from that last hand, that we will have many more."

Quark glanced at the chips. Naralak's pile was twice that of the others on the table.

"I'm keeping my eye on you," Klar said. He poured himself another cup of saki. "The kind of luck you've been having tonight is rare."

"Now, now," Quark said, bobbing just a little, careful not to disturb the remaining drinks on his tray. "These are practice games. They should have no bearing on tomorrow."

"Trust me," Naralak said. "The only bearing they'll have is by showing us early how poorly our opponents play." She smiled at Klar as she spoke. He did not smile back.

Quark moved away from them to the next table. Pera, the Bajoran, had a large pile of chips in front of him. He had a quirky half smile and a series of small

white scars that ran down the side of his face—
product of Cardassian torture. Pera claimed that he
was never part of any terrorist group but his scars
belied it. Quark put the sherry down in front of him
and more Romulan ale in front of his companions.

The two Romulan men, Darak and Kinsak, were as
well-known for their tempers as for their poker-
playing skills. They had already yelled at Quark for
allowing Klingons to play. He had told them that
anyone could play regardless of race, as long as they
had enough credentials and gold-pressed latinum.

At the edge of the table, the Sligiloid sat alone. She
was tall and slender, and covered with thin blue
scales. Rom had brushed her when taking her name,
and her skin had flashed with a brilliant blue light. She
had also cussed him out in her native tongue so
harshly that Rom had refused to go near her again.

"Nothing for me, Mr. Quark?" asked the human
woman sitting just behind Klar. Quark smiled at her.
He had had his eye on her since she arrived. She wore
a diaphanous pink gown that revealed more of her
voluptuous figure than it concealed. She also carried a
tribble, which had caused some stir when she came
through the docking bay. Odo had refused to allow her
on the station until Dr. Bashir made sure the cooing
blond furball was sterile.

"I'm sorry, Miss Jones," Quark said, hovering over
her. If he craned his neck slightly, he got a good view
of her cleavage. "You didn't order anything."

"Hmm," she said, leaning back. "The Romulan ale
looks good."

Quark leaned forward. He could see all the way to
her navel. "Yes," he said. "Looks good."

A hand slapped his back—hard—sending pain all

the way to his toes. Quark stood up. A tall, balding human stood behind him, a smile on his uneven features. Berlinghoff Rasmussen. He was known throughout the galaxy for the scams he pulled, starting with the one he tried on the *Enterprise* crew when he arrived from the past, claiming he was from the future. "I think the lady wanted a beverage," Rasmussen said.

Quark nodded, once. He didn't want to tangle with his guests so early in the festivities. "Romulan ale. Anything for you, sir?"

Rasmussen paused, then grinned. "I would like a beer as well, but a human beer. Make that Irish, from the late nineteenth century—a stout—and serve it warm."

Quark grimaced. He hated drinkers with a palate. "Would you like it from a wooden barrel with a cork, or a tin barrel with a stopper?"

"Very good!" Rasmussen said. "But not quite right. Storage became an issue in the twentieth century—"

"You getting drinks?" asked a male voice behind Quark.

He turned to it as quickly as he could. Rasmussen was known to carry on a conversation past its death. The man sitting at the table with the Romulans was small and dark, with a thick beard and dark hair on his arms and back. Sergei Davidovich. "I would like Anubian vodka. Bring the bottle."

"Yes, sir," Quark said. He left the table as quickly as he could. He stood in the center of the room and snapped his fingers. From the main bar, the Dabo girl rolled her eyes at him, but she came to his summons.

When she was beside him, he whispered the drink orders to her.

"They're not going to smell, are they?" she asked, glancing at the remaining table.

Quark followed her gaze. The Meepod, a five-armed, soft-skinned creature, had just finished her drink. The Klingons beside her were still sipping theirs. "Not if you hurry," Quark said.

The Dabo girl scurried out of the room. Quark took a deep breath and headed for the remaining table. He already saw trouble. Two Klingon men—Xator and Grouk—sat with their backs to the first table Quark had stopped at. Directly behind them, with her back turned, was Naralak. Quark twisted his hands together. He knew that he would have to face having Romulans and Klingons play against each other, but he wasn't looking forward to it. At the last major poker tournament in the quadrant, two Klingons had died at the hands of Romulans.

Still, Quark couldn't do anything without calling attention to the problem. He would just have to worry about it in silence. Besides, one of his ringers, Baun, sat at the table. His pile of chips was dishearteningly small. Quark sighed. Tomorrow everything would work better.

Much, much better.

Rom ran into the room, carrying the drink order Quark had given to the Dabo girl. Quark frowned. He would have to yell at her for making Rom do her job. The Dabo girl caught Quark's gaze, waved three fingers on her right hand, and closed the door to the back room.

Fine. She couldn't be any clearer about her unwillingness to do her job.

A handful of other players mingled. Two more Klingons—those trouble-making women from the

House of Duras—conversed with a long-haired Freepery. His other ringer, Nam, was trying to corner a human woman near the buffet table. A tentacled Totozoid, who had requested half hour breaks so that it could wet its gills, dripped on the carpet near the door.

"Quite the crowd."

Quark didn't have to look up. The voice belonged to Rasmussen. Again. Quark sighed silently. He would have to put up with the man for the next few days. "Yes," Quark said, "and not everyone is here yet."

"I'm amazed at the folks who are," Rasmussen said. "Naralak who is known for her by-the-numbers cheating system. Darak and Kinsak who haven't been in a room with Naralak since the Great Poker Shootout on Risa two years ago. Pera, known for smuggling anything, as long as it profits Bajor—"

"I'm familiar with all these players," Quark said.

"Then I'm surprised you invited them," Rasmussen said. He smiled that goofy half-grin that Quark always wanted to wipe from his face. "I mean, everyone knows that Cynthia Jones can't abide Grabansters. They *eat* tribbles, for heaven's sake. Klingons and Romulans in the same room. Good thing Cardassians aren't here, what with Pera—"

"Wait until tomorrow," Quark said. He weaved away from Rasmussen. Quark knew about the tensions, and he knew things that Rasmussen probably didn't know—that Harding was wanted for assault on Sift IV, and that Sergei Davidovich beheaded the Irits' podmate during the final moments of a heated Seven Card High Low game in the Miridious Belt. He merely hoped that the players would forget their differences in the thick of the game.

Rom hurried over to Quark, tray at his side. "The Meepod wants another drink," Rom whispered loudly. "And that Dabo girl refuses to serve any more."

Just as Quark turned to Rom, the room went dark. The words Quark was about to say about firing that Dabo girl died in his throat.

The station rocked and Quark had to grab a chair to keep his balance.

Curses in a dozen different languages flew around the room.

Alarms wailed from the corridors.

Quark tried to stare through the darkness. What was going on? Was the station under attack? He heard no announcements, had seen no preparation. No one had said anything to him. Sisko would hear about this! Sisko and the entire Federation!

The rocking slowed. Quark regained his balance and took a deep breath. Maybe they had just hit something. Maybe it was some internal problem. Maybe it was nothing at all. Just a momentary glitch.

Quark wiped a hand over his brow. The automatic temperature controls must have gone out as well. The room had suddenly grown stifling hot.

The wet-dog smell of the Grabanster became overpowering in the heat. Beneath it, Quark thought he caught a whiff of smoke. Panic rose in his stomach. He pushed the feeling down.

This was the worst thing that could happen. The worst. Rumor would spread across the sector that Quark's was a low-life dive that couldn't even host a proper tournament.

"Please, everyone," Quark shouted above the noise. "Remain in your places. The emergency lights will come on in a moment." He hoped. He wasn't even sure the bar had emergency lights.

He reached out and grabbed to his left, hoping Rom had not moved. The flesh his fingers found was ridged and cool. And familiar. He yanked Rom close to his face. "Find O'Brien," Quark whispered with as much force as he could. "I want to know what is going on. Nothing can be allowed to disrupt the game."

"But I can't see any more than you can," Rom said. His voice almost had a human whine. Rom had picked up too many habits from the Federation do-gooders who filled the station. Before, the Cardassians had been teaching Rom proper, treacherous manners.

"I don't care if you can see or not," Quark said. "Just go." He shoved Rom hard in the direction of the door. He heard Rom crash into a chair and swear. Another voice rose in a curse and something crashed again, before Quark heard the hiss of the door. Good. Rom would find O'Brien and get this place working again.

A drop of sweat rolled in the ridges of Quark's brow, itching something fierce. "Please just stay calm," he said, hoping to quiet the protests. "It won't be long now."

"It better not be," a female voice said. Another female squealed and a slap resounded in the darkness.

The alarms sounded like screams outside the door. Beside him, the Grabanster chattered constantly. Quark felt like telling it to shut up, but he had seen the color of its gold-pressed latinum. No sense in angering a customer before a big game.

"You touched my cards," a deep, accented voice said. Quark couldn't tell if the voice was male or female, Ferengi or alien. He hated this blackness. He tried to move toward the voice. He didn't want any accusations of cheating before the game began.

"Why would I do that?" The responding voice had a flat accent that made Quark think of Earth-raised humans. "I can't see your cards any more than I can see you."

The voices were coming from an area behind Quark. Everyone else had quieted. Except for the alarms, honking like a Davesian goose.

"Just keep your hands to yourself," the first voice said. "Or I—"

"Gentlemen, gentlemen," Quark said, hoping he had the gender right. The table was in his way. His feet banged into a chair and someone growled. "Please. The lights will be back on in a moment and we will start the hands over again."

"I said, keep your hands off my cards."

A chair fell back with a clatter, then something crashed through a table. Quark closed his eyes. His beautiful game. Voices rose, screaming and yelling in a dozen languages. The chattering beside him sounded almost like a rat screaming.

Another chair clattered, then another, and the thud of fists hitting flesh filled the room. Quark grabbed a scaly arm, and the Sligiloid flashed a brilliant blue light that showed the room in a strobelike instant: Twenty-two humans and aliens clustered around the tables. Some beings were standing, but most were sitting. Baun clutched his cards to his chest, his smaller-than-typical ears twitching. Good. He was guarding his cards even in a pickup game.

The Sligiloid slurped. The sound was not friendly. Quark edged away. The smell of sulfur filled the air as the strobe light faded. The thudding sounds continued. The moment of light had not illuminated any fighting.

Quark snaked around the Sligiloid, careful not to touch it again—touching them made them angry— and followed the sound. He tripped on another chair just as the lights came back on.

Quark blinked at the brightness. The bead of sweat caught in his brow ridges fell into his right eye, burning it. He rubbed at it anxiously as he scanned the room.

Near the door, one table had fallen, and all the chairs around it were down. Sergei Davidovich and the Meepod were sprawled on the floor. The Meepod was slugging Davidovich, but he was giving as good as he got, using his long legs as leverage while he butted his head against the Meepod's belly.

"Stop them," Quark shouted at the scuffle. The Klingon, Xator, and the Romulan, Kinsak, pulled the fighters apart. Then Xator growled at Kinsak. Kinsak's eyebrows narrowed and his mouth rose in a sneer. Quark hurried over and placed himself between them all. "Thank you," he said, pushing the groups away from each other. "Thank you very much."

Davidovich's face was bloody and half of his beard had been pulled away. The Meepod had turned green. Quark couldn't remember her name, only that it was unpronounceable. "I should ban you both from the game," he said. Putting the idea of cheating in the heads of the other players. It would make his job so much tougher now. They would all be watchful.

The Meepod wiped black ichor from her stomach, clearing the mouth that hid in the folds of flesh around what would be a chest on a Ferengi. She was standing free. Kinsak had let her go to protect himself from Xator. "But he was fixing my hand," the Meepod said in her deep voice. "I could feel it."

"How could I do that? We weren't even at the same table!" Davidovich said. Xator held him like a shield and continued to growl at Kinsak.

"Then you were cheating for someone!" the Meepod said. "I felt your hairy arm on my skin."

Quark made sure he remained between Davidovich and the Meepod. The Meepod's black ichor had a rotting flesh smell. Another drop of sweat caught in Quark's brow ridges. "Stop it," he said. "I will not have this sort of behavior in my place. Is that understood?"

"Quark!" Baun shouted from the back of the room.

Stupid ringer. Didn't he know that he shouldn't call attention to himself? Someone might suspect that Baun worked for Quark.

"I'm busy," Quark said without turning around.

"Quark!"

The rest of the room had become quiet. Even Xator had stopped growling at Kinsak. The alarms outside had shut down, leaving a ringing in Quark's ears. The sweat dropped off his brow ridge and landed in his left eye. Now both eyes stung.

"Quark!"

Quark had heard this tone in Baun's voice before. Those moments when Baun went from wide-eyed innocent to competent cardplayer. Something had happened.

Slowly Quark turned to look. Naralak was slumped in her chair, her squinty eyes forever opened on the world. Her green blood mingled with the lovely green felt on the table in front of her. More blood spattered the wall and the surrounding chairs. Baun stood beside her, his hand on her shoulder. One of Quark's specialty cutting knives, used only for Ferengi Cold Ilami dishes, stuck out of her chest.

"I thought," Baun said, "that I could help her, but she had already been gone too long."

The Klingons gathered around like Sturgan vultures. "She looks much better now," B'Etor from the House of Duras said.

"Did you touch her?" Quark asked Baun, trying to keep the hope out of his voice. If Baun had touched her, then that would solve two problems: It would get Baun out of the game now that he had called attention to himself and give the players a patsy so the game could continue uninterrupted. Then Quark could get a new ringer, someone who was a bit more discreet.

"Quark," Baun said with that patronizing tone Quark hated, "there is no sense in touching a body that is so fully and completely dead."

The remaining Romulans stood at the side of the table opposite the Klingons. The Romulans stared at the dead woman. "If you killed her, Klingon," Kinsak said, "I will make sure that our government knows of your crime."

Lursa laughed. "As if you're on speaking terms with the Romulan government."

The Irits peered over the table. "This . . . is . . . most . . . un-for-tu-nate," it said. "Perhaps . . . there . . . is . . . a . . . kil-ler . . . that . . . has . . . lost . . . its . . . mind. We . . . will . . . all . . . die."

"We will not die!" Quark said. How stupid. His players don't need to think about that on top of everything else. "This was just an accident."

"A very convenient accident," the Meepod said.

"Well, you didn't help much," Quark snapped.

22

"How do I know your fight wasn't providing cover for someone?"

The Meepod drew herself to her full height, even though the movement was clearly painful. "Meepods never help anyone," she said.

"I do think we have a problem here," said Cynthia Jones. Her tribble hadn't made a sound. "We can't play tomorrow with a dead body in the room."

"Quite right." Quark swallowed, and made his way around the tables to the dead Romulan. The blood had soaked into the felt—the stain wasn't *that* noticeable—but someone would have to scrub the walls. Poor Rom. Quark hoped his brother didn't have plans for the evening, because those plans would have to be canceled.

"Of course, we will have to notify Odo," Baun said. "I think—"

"You think too much," Quark hissed. Then he smiled. "Of course I will notify Chief of Security Odo." Just much later, he thought.

Quark smiled at those gathered around. "The game will continue tomorrow as scheduled. You have all traveled much too far to let a little problem like this set you back."

"We're going to play with a killer on the loose?" Baun asked.

If Quark could have kicked Baun, he would have. "Gamblers never let anything get in the way of a game." The men at the table nodded. "Of course, you could resign, Baun. I'm sure I could find another to take your place."

Baun frowned. No one else seemed terribly upset by the turn of events. Kinsak was still focused on Xator, and Darak, the other Romulan, was pointedly staring at his cards. It seemed that Naralak didn't even have friends among her own kind. What luck. Quark suppressed a smile. He loved professional gamblers.

"Well," Baun said slowly. "If that's the way it's done . . ." He slumped into the empty seat. "You will tell Odo, won't you, Quark?"

"Of course," Quark said. In his own good time, though, *after* the tournament was over. Now all he had to do was to hide the body, and the players would forget the commotion.

He wished Rom was back. His good-for-nothing brother was never around when Quark needed him. Quark would have to carry the body to the storage room himself. He couldn't ask Baun. That would prove that Baun worked for him.

Quark frowned. He'd always wanted to touch a Romulan woman, but not like this. He bent over the body and grabbed hold of Naralak's arms.

"Don't you think you should wait for . . . ?" Baun asked.

"He'll see it soon enough," Quark snapped. He shoved his shoulder in Naralak's stomach and lifted her. Her blood was sticky and smelt faintly of copper. He felt it seep into his new sweater—the one he had saved especially for this occasion. Her hands and feet scraped the ground. She was heavy. Ferengi women never got that heavy.

He closed his eyes. He had to remember all the money he would make. That kind of profit made anything possible. Then he opened his eyes and started toward the storage room. Each step elicited a small grunt from the back of his throat.

He was three steps away from the door when it hissed open. He looked up.

Odo was framed in the doorway, his usual frown on his half-formed face.

Suddenly the weight on his shoulders felt twenty times heavier.

"Well, well," Odo said, sending chills through Quark's body. "What have we here?"

CHAPTER
3

CHIEF ENGINEER O'BRIEN tugged the shirt of his uniform as he hurried to Ops. A man needed—rest—every now and then. Was it his fault that Keiko had come to their quarters at the same time? He hadn't seen his wife in almost two days, since their rotations didn't match, and Molly was off at a friend's for the afternoon. He had taken off his communications badge and set it on a chair in the bathroom with the rest of his clothes. Not a crime, really. After all, he was supposed to have twenty-four hours off. And of course he hadn't noticed the flickering lights. No lights had been on in their quarters. Kira had no right to be angry with him. He had been on his own time.

The unpainted girders in the corridor looked strange in the thin light. His ears still rang from the alarms, and Kira's curt scolding. He was not at her beck and call. He would tell her that if she gave him a hard time in Ops.

He would have enough to deal with, judging by that last power outage.

It had caught him just outside his quarters. In the darkness and in his sleepy state, he had gotten confused for a moment and thought he was in a corridor on the *Enterprise*. No such luck. The *Enterprise* at its worst never achieved the level of engineering disaster O'Brien dealt with each day in the Deep Space Nine. And, judging from Kira's tone, that level of disaster had suddenly grown measurably worse.

Outside the turbolift a Ferengi and a humanoid escorted an ancient Ferengi down the corridor. The Nagus. As if the engineering problems weren't enough. O'Brien nodded at them, trying to not stare at the fine white hairs growing out of the Nagus's oversized ears. The Ferengi made him nervous. Their unabashed avarice made him feel as if they ran naked in public. Such blatant emotion grated against his own conservative upbringing.

The turbolift had the dry, almost mothball-like scent that Ferengi seemed to prefer. Mixed with the smell of burnt wiring and a rising heat which could only mean that the environmental controls were down again. O'Brien really didn't want to get on. But he did. He hoped by the time the lift reached Ops the headache threatening behind his eyes would disappear.

As he expected, Ops was a mess. A thin haze of smoke filled the room, filtering everything through a gray gauze. Most of the smoke gathered at the top of Ops, near the portals, blocking O'Brien's favorite view. The burnt electrical smell was stronger here, and some wires still sparked near the transporter unit behind his desk. Everything was dark in Sisko's office—something that should never happen. Lights blinked on every visible panel.

Sisko manned one station, while Dax huddled over the science console. Sisko glanced up and nodded, not saying a word as O'Brien scrambled to his engineering station.

Kira stood up from behind the station. When she saw O'Brien, her brown eyes narrowed. "We could have used you earlier, mister."

Half a dozen more lights lit up on his board as he stood there. He didn't have time to make excuses or to fight with the major. He stepped in front of her and bent over his console.

Most of the major systems, including all power and life support, were running for the moment. But it was going to take him most of the day to recalibrate some of the smaller systems and processors. Nothing that couldn't wait until he figured out what had caused all this in the first place.

"I've got what is left of the Ferengi ship," Dax said, as if she were continuing a conversation. The sound of her low, calm voice made him realize how silent Ops really was. "It's in a safe orbit away from the station. It will hold there for salvage."

Ferengi ship? A lot had happened since he went to his quarters. "The Ferengi caused this?" O'Brien asked.

Sisko did not look up. "Whatever bounced us around destroyed their ship. We tried to grab it, but the tractor beam cut out."

One more problem. But a bit of relief as well. The in-station malfunctions happened because of an outside event. O'Brien had been afraid that with the

Cardassian systems and his jury-rigging, some important connector he didn't even know about had blown.

"You don't know what happened?" O'Brien asked.

"No," Kira snapped. She was at another station, paging for more help on the bridge. "But whatever hit us had to be big. A wide area was affected."

"Any idea how wide?" Maybe if he knew the source, it would help him determine the quickest way to solve the problems.

"We have had reports from as far away as Bajor," Dax said.

"Any fix as to location? Or source?" O'Brien asked.

Dax shook her head. "At this point I don't even know *what* hit us."

"Well," O'Brien said, "perhaps the damage will give us a clue. We can eliminate a number of possibilities just by looking at the destruction pattern."

"Do it," Sisko said.

"We need to have systems up and running first," Kira said. O'Brien would never get used to the blunt rudeness of Bajoran women. He had often wondered why Sisko, a Starfleet commander, had not insisted that she use more formal address.

"Well, then, Major," Sisko said, humor lacing his deep voice. "I guess you'll have to investigate the damage yourself."

O'Brien suppressed a smile as he told the computer to trace system malfunctions and separate out the work assignments. If he could pass the easy stuff to some of his support staff, he could worry about the larger problems, like the tractor beam.

He rubbed his forehead. The smoke was making that headache worse, and a tickle grew in the back of his throat. Maybe he would work on the replicators first. He needed coffee.

"Call coming in from the Cardassians," Kira said.

The hair on the back of O'Brien's neck tingled. Cardassians. Would they know a way to disable the station without being traced? He punched in three diagnostic programs with that scenario in mind.

"Put them on the main viewscreen," Sisko said. He stood and walked to the operations table. A Cardassian face O'Brien had never seen before dominated the main viewscreen. The Cardassian's ridges and lines, wide eyes, and down-turned mouth made O'Brien very, very uneasy.

"I am Commander Benjamin Sisko, Captain." Sisko's voice had grown deeper, more authoritative. "I run Deep Space Nine."

"I am familiar with you, Sisko." The captain did not introduce himself. "I want to know if your assault on our ships was intentional."

"I can assure you that we had nothing to do with any attack on your ships. Check your sensors and you'll see that the interruption happened in a wide section of space near the wormhole. We were affected as well."

"We read no significant damage to your station, Commander," the Cardassian said. "We, on the other hand, have had two ships knocked off-line, and a power core disruption in another. All evidence points to a subspace distortion that came from this system. Explain this."

"I wish we could," Sisko said. "We lost lights and power a few moments ago."

The Cardassian pushed his face closer to the screen.

"We have kept our agreement with the Federation, despite incursions by Bajoran terrorists and the increased activity caused by the wormhole. The agreement is no longer binding when you attack our fleet."

O'Brien gripped the edge of the console. The Cardassians could get ugly when they were angry. Sisko put his hands behind his back and took a deep breath.

"We did not attack your fleet. Something affected us both. We are doing what we can to discover the cause."

The Cardassian's smile did not reach his eyes. "Do that, Commander. And I hope your explanation is a good one. But let me warn you. If these attacks continue it will be perceived as an act of war."

The viewscreen went blank. Sisko frowned. He turned to Dax. "The affected area must have been larger than we suspected."

His calmness surprised O'Brien. But then, Sisko had never experienced the full wrath of the Cardassians.

O'Brien studied the board in front of him. The diagnostics had shown no evidence of Cardassian attack. In fact, the first diagnostic found no cause at all.

The lights flickered.

O'Brien did not glance up. Maybe if he ignored the lights, the problems would go away. The second diagnostic he ran showed that all the replicators were off-line, as well as the environmental controls in Ops, the Promenade, and most of the docking ring.

"Benjamin," Dax said, "I am getting a strange subspace surge. I can't seem to pinpoint it, but . . ."

She stopped talking for a moment as her fingers flew over the board in front of her. "The sensors have gone dead."

"O'Brien?" Sisko said.

The headache had spread in a tight band around his skull. A hundred warning lights flared into being. The diagnostics stopped as the system overloaded. Everything was just going wrong at once—again.

The lights flickered.

Then the station rocked as another wave hit it and the inertial dampers cut out for a moment. In his bed, the wave had felt like an earthquake, but here it felt as if a giant had grabbed the station and shook it in his overlarge hands. O'Brien clung to the engineering console and kept an eye on the sparking connectors near the transporter.

When the rocking stopped, he rerouted power from some backup systems in time to stop another total blackout. A bit more rerouting, and some of the warning lights went out. Except one very important one. The station's power core containment had been slightly damaged. He did a quick run-through of the core systems, checking every detail until he was satisfied everything was fine.

Ops was stifling hot, and the tickle in his throat had grown worse. He permitted himself a small cough before turning to Dax. "Sensors back up?"

Dax nodded.

"We lost the transporters and half the station's turbolifts on that one," O'Brien said. "And there was slight damage to power core containment. I have that under control."

Sisko nodded. "Start with the turbolifts and get

everything back up as soon as you can. Dax, can you tell how widespread that one was?"

"There is nothing to measure, Benjamin."

"Another message coming in from the Cardassians," Kira said. "They don't sound happy."

No one was happy. O'Brien least of all. "If the Cardassians got hit again," O'Brien said, "we're dealing with something really big."

And not very discriminating. After the turbolifts, he would work on the replicators. He had a hunch coffee would grow in importance as the hours wore on.

CHAPTER
4

THE FLICKERING LIGHTS reminded Odo, Chief of Station Security, of the last days of the Cardassian reign. While the station rumbled and shook, he sat on his chair, letting it bounce around while he maintained his dignity. Lieutenant George Primmon, Starfleet Security, who was sitting across from him, had gone pale in that delightfully unconscious way humans had of showing fear. Primmon wasn't as tough as he thought he was. He had actually stifled a cry when the lights went out this last time.

Odo sighed with impatience. In his hand he held a printout of a communiqué from Starfleet. The communiqué had come to Primmon, and Odo had noted, even before the lights went out, that it was incomplete. Now that the lights had returned, he scanned the document. It said nothing of any use.

He waited until the alarm sirens went off before continuing the conversation. He could have spoken over the noise, but no sense straining himself. Besides, he didn't want to put Primmon at ease.

"So," Odo said as if the conversation had never stopped. "Who is this L'sthwan?"

Primmon's Adam's apple bobbed as he swallowed. He ran his palms over the legs of his uniform, as if he were trying to put himself back together. "Don't you want to check with Sisko and see what the problem is?"

"If it concerned me, he would have contacted me," Odo said. "Obviously the problem is technical, and that falls into Chief O'Brien's area." Odo leaned forward and put his elbows on his desk. "You were going to tell me about L'sthwan?"

Primmon shot a nervous glance at the door. Through it Odo could see people in the Promenade, hurrying to get out of the public areas before the station's lights went down again.

"L'sthwan?" Primmon said, as if he had already forgotten. His Adam's apple bobbed again. The man was not only officious. He was afraid of the dark. Primmon took a deep breath. "I have never dealt with the man personally. He is a compulsive gambler, and unlike most, he's excellent at it. He also kills. He started out in the Vukcevich Sector, where gossip attributes fifteen deaths to his hand. He's also wanted for murder in the Hoffman colonies. Oltion Four has a warrant out for him—seems he murdered an entire family just after supper and the Oltonions want to execute him for it. He was caught red-handed in the Patterson Belt, murdering a companion over a game of cards. Four guards showed up and L'sthwan killed them too—only the last one lived long enough to send a communiqué to the district commander. Unfortunately, no one ever got a complete description of L'sthwan, and he has always managed to achieve a quick escape. Starfleet considers him dangerous."

"Obviously," Odo said. "Or they wouldn't have sent *you* to protect us."

"I am not here to protect—" Primmon stopped himself and jutted out his chin, realizing a beat too late that Odo was being sarcastic. "I served many years on starships. Problems like these often lead to bigger things."

"So instead you moved into a comfortable job and spend your time harassing me."

"Look, Constable, the Federation wants L'sthwan. He's dangerous—"

"—even the communiqué says that," Odo said, the sarcasm making his words sound flat.

"—and Starfleet doesn't need any problems from you."

"No," Odo said. "You need my help. You complain about my efficiency, and you give me nothing to work with. A communiqué. A name. Personality traits that could describe half the customers at Quark's. If you give me something to work with then maybe I will give you results."

"We know he's here."

"Do you? The communiqué says nothing about that."

Primmon shrugged. "The Federation would not have sent me to you without a reason."

"Of course they would," Odo said.

Primmon's face lost its paleness. A bright red flush was working its way up his neck to his chin. Odo loved that flush. It was visible proof that he angered

Primmon as much as Primmon angered him. "I'll get his record sent from the Federation."

"Good," Odo said. "By the time it arrives, L'sthwan will have left."

The flush had made its way to Primmon's eyebrows. He stood. "I would check Quark's if I were you. If L'sthwan is on the station, he will be there."

"Brilliant," Odo said. "You want me to search for a man I don't know, who could be using a different name, who is human or humanoid, and a gambler. Do you suggest I arrest half of the clientele?"

"I suggest you interview Quark. Quark may know him." The flush had reached the roots of Primmon's hair.

"Indeed," Odo said. "And Quark will turn one of his paying customers over to me. It astounds me how little you know of the Ferengi mind."

"Odo." Primmon's voice raised a notch.

Odo stood. "I will go to Quark's because I planned to go there anyway. Have you noticed how few people are in the Promenade?"

Primmon glanced out through the door's glass. He shrugged. "With all the technical problems, they're probably staying on their ships or in their quarters. It makes sense to me."

His tone implied that he would like to be off the station too. Odo nodded. Of course Primmon didn't notice the real problem. People like Primmon never did. Instead, he wanted Odo to search for a murderous gambler at Quark's, which was something like searching for a scout ship in the wormhole: one was always easy to find, but not the right one. Odo shoved past Primmon and opened the door for him.

Primmon paused in front of him. "Why did you ask me that?"

Odo stared at him, wondering how the man had ever worked in security. "Because the docking rings are nearly full. Most of the ships have arrived in the last twenty-four hours. Crews usually shop in the Promenade. When there are that many ships, the station is crowded. It's not."

"You think that's significant?"

"I'm going to find out," Odo said. He escorted Primmon out the door, which closed behind them. Primmon headed toward his quarters. Odo turned toward Quark's.

He had checked the duty rosters on all the ships that had docked and found that most had given their crews shore leave on Bajor. The makeup of the crews seemed odd to him as well. Most of them had little or no experience, while others were known for their smuggling and nefarious dealings. When Primmon had said the word "gambler," Odo had been way ahead of him.

But Odo had seen nothing unusual at Quark's. If anything, the number of players at the Dabo tables had been down the last few nights. Still, an uneasy feeling had grown in Odo's stomach and that uneasy feeling usually meant Quark was up to something.

As he approached Quark's, he stopped. No noise. No laughter. No shouts of "Dabo!" True, the problems at the station might have affected the clientele, as Primmon suggested, but it never had before. Everyone played at Quark's whether there was a problem or not.

Two Bajoran men argued quietly at a table in the center of the bar. The Dabo girl leaned on the Dabo table, holding her stick and moving the pieces herself.

She smiled when she saw Odo, then the smile faded when she realized who he was.

The bar smelled faintly of wet dog, and the climate controls were out. The heat was enough to drive anyone away, apparantly even Quark who, contrary to his norm, was nowhere to be found. Neither was Rom. Quark never left the bar unattended. Odo scanned the upper tables. Not even Nog showed his young Ferengi face.

"Is your boss here?" Odo asked the Dabo girl.

She glanced at the door leading into the back room, then at the table, her gaze never touching Odo. "No," she said. "He left me in charge."

Very strange. Quark wouldn't trust the profits of his bar to anyone, let alone a non-Ferengi. Which meant that the profits were being made elsewhere. The back room? Quark used it for special games, private playing sessions, and occasional auctions. "You're in charge," Odo said.

The Dabo girl nodded.

"In charge of sending clients into that back room?"

Again, that quick glance. She turned the Dabo stick over in her fingers. "No," she said quietly. "I can use the replicator just as well as anyone else."

"I bet you can," Odo said. He pushed past her and strode across the room to the big door that led into the back room. The Dabo girl touched his arm, but he shook her off. The door hissed open, revealing ten tables covered with green felt, about twenty clients— human, alien, and Ferengi—and Quark, his body half hidden under the weight of a Romulan woman. Her hair brushed the floor, her hands and feet dragged on it, and her green blood covered half of Quark's shirt.

She had to be dead. No living woman, let alone a Romulan, would let Quark touch her like that.

"What have we here?" Odo asked.

Quark peeked from under the Romulan's armpit, took a deep breath of air and seemed to hold it. "I can explain," he said.

"I certainly hope so," Odo replied.

CHAPTER
5

THE STATION'S POWER OUTAGES had taken the environmental controls off-line. Dr. Julian Bashir pushed his shirtsleeves over his elbows. He had created a stasis field over the body of the dead Romulan woman, but once that was broken, he would have only a few minutes to conduct the autopsy. The heat would begin the process of decay even quicker, and that much blood would attract some of the more interesting staph infections onto the body's surface.

To make matters worse, Odo and Primmon, the Starfleet security officer, were hovering over the body, as if it were a prize to be given to the best detective. Bashir wiped his forehead, then went to the counter and sterilized his hands.

"I don't want either of you close to that body," he said. "We'll have enough troubles as it is."

Both men backed up. No matter what they thought of Bashir outside of the infirmary, inside he was God.

He was about to remove the stasis field when the door hissed open.

"I told you to run the sterilization program in the other room," he snapped without looking up. New assistants often had to hear instructions twice before completing them.

"Then I didn't hear you correctly, Doctor." The answering voice was deep and warm, with a trace of humor. Bashir felt a heat that had nothing to do with the environmental controls run through his body.

He whirled. Commander Benjamin Sisko stood at the door, hands clasped behind his back, his normally trim uniform marred with smoke stains on one sleeve. "Commander, I didn't realize—"

"I know," Sisko said with a smile. Then he approached the body, and frowned. "Have you found anything?"

"I need to do a blood and urine analysis, and a DNA scan," Bashir said, "but I can already tell you that the cause of death is exactly what it appears to be: five stab wounds. Three to the stomach, one to the left lung. The fifth wound killed her: it punctured the heart."

"Then what are you completing the other scans for?" Sisko asked.

"There was a bit of material on the knife that I didn't recognize," Bashir said. "I'll do a poison analysis, as well as a fiber trace. The knife had no prints. It was a Ferengi knife, the kind they use for some of their more grotesque cold dishes."

Sisko looked at the body. Bashir followed his gaze, trying to see with Sisko's eyes. The woman was now nude. The stab wounds had discolored her greenish tinted skin, leaving large bruised areas along her torso. Her eyes were still open, haunted, empty. Her black hair was swept back, revealing swooping eyebrows and small, pointed ears. She had had a kind of beauty.

"Who did this?" Sisko asked. When no one responded, he turned his head slightly toward Odo. "Why did someone die on my station?"

Bashir moved to the other side of the body and removed the stasis field. He wanted to be as far from Sisko as possible. Something in Sisko's voice let Bashir know that the commander would not tolerate any uncertainties.

"It seems our dear friend Quark has decided to hold a poker tournament," Odo said, "and has invited every undesirable he can find from inside and outside the Federation."

"Actually, sir," Primmon said, "we have a suspect. His name is L'sthwan. Starfleet sent us a communiqué telling us to watch for him. He is a noted gambler and murderer, wanted on Starbase Five for—"

"If we have a suspect," Sisko said, "why isn't he in custody?"

The metallic odor of blood rose from the body so strongly that Bashir had to step back. He programmed the computer to run a scan while he removed blood traces for later examination. Even though he was working, he was listening.

"What Mr. Primmon didn't tell you, Commander," Odo said, his voice even flatter than usual, "is that Starfleet's communiqué is extremely vague. They warn us about L'sthwan, but do not tell us his age, race, or appearance. They don't even know for sure if he will be on Deep Space Nine. Mr. Primmon has assumed—"

"I don't want assumptions," Sisko snapped. "I want answers."

"Here is what we know so far," Odo said. "The door to Quark's back room was closed just before the big power outage. The computer tells us that the door opened and closed once in the darkness and that no one beamed in. I have run a preliminary DNA trace and fiber scan, matching the information against the thirty people in the room, and have found nothing unusual. But I am sure that someone in that room killed her."

"Wonderful. One chance in thirty of catching a killer." Sisko stood over the body. He was staring at Bashir's hands. Bashir tried not to look up. He didn't want his hands to shake. "I want no ship to leave this station until the murderer is caught. Close down Quark's poker game and let me know as soon as you have something."

Bashir finished running the diagnostics. He reinstated the stasis field until he could put the body into cold storage. "Do you really think shutting down the game is such a good idea?" he asked. "After all, the murderer came here to play poker."

"The doctor has a point," Odo said. "I would love to shut down Quark's little game, but I think we have a better chance of catching the killer if the game goes on."

"Do you have a plan, Odo?" Sisko asked.

"With all due respect, sir." Primmon imposed his small frame between Sisko and Odo. "If the game continues, the killer might kill again. I think any plan the constable has will be a poor one."

"The killer will not kill again," Odo said, "because I will have joined the game."

Bashir frowned. He crossed his arms in front of his chest. "I didn't know you gambled."

"I don't," Odo said. "But I am willing to do what I must to catch a killer."

"Sir." Primmon leaned against the autopsy table. Bashir tapped his shoulder and moved him away. Primmon grimaced at him. Bashir resisted the urge to grimace back. The man was difficult, but making faces at him would not impress the commander. "I would like to advise against this action."

"Mr. Primmon," Sisko said, his voice firm, "we have had this discussion before. Odo is highly qualified to do his job. If he believes that his plan will flush our killer, then I believe it will as well." Sisko stepped around Primmon so that Primmon was excluded from the conversation. "Odo, will Quark let you into the tournament?"

"I can handle Quark," Odo said.

Sisko nodded. "I believe you can."

Bashir moved away from the table. He envied Odo, spending his time at the poker game, even with a killer on the loose. This was the kind of frontier that Bashir had imagined. He had begged Quark to let him into the game, but Quark had repeatedly said no. He believed that Bashir wouldn't be able to hold his own. But Bashir had always done well in late night games in the Academy Medical School, and knew he would be able to now.

"Dr. Bashir," Sisko said. "If you find anything unusual in the remaining lab work, notify me immediately."

The commander's curt tones snapped Bashir from his reverie. "Yes, sir," he said.

Sisko glanced at the Romulan woman on the table and then back at Odo. "Find whoever did this."

Odo nodded. "I will. That you can count on."

The lights flickered. The stasis field fluctuated and disappeared. Bashir hurried back to the table to reestablish the field.

Sisko glanced up at the overhead light and then back at Odo. "Good," he said. "At the moment we need something around here we can count on."

CHAPTER
6

Odo loved to hear Quark whimper.

And Quark had been doing just that for the past fifteen minutes. The temperature in Odo's office had risen since the last power outage, and the sharp, fermented smell of Ferengi sweat filled the room. Beads of moisture dripped off Quark's brow ridges onto his nose. Some traveled around the rims of his oversized ears. Quark swatted at the drops as if they were Bajoran liccie bugs.

Odo stood over Quark, hoping to make the Ferengi even more nervous. Quark made mistakes when he was nervous. He kept glancing over his shoulder at the door. The Promenade was still empty and Quark's place was not visible from Odo's office.

"If you aren't going to ask questions, you should let me go," Quark said. The left side of his clothing was stained with the Romulan's blood.

"Oh, I plan to ask questions." Odo paused for

maximum effect. He had avoided questioning Quark, hoping the tension would make Quark more talkative. Quark had hovered around Odo in the back room while they waited for Bashir to arrive. Once the doctor took the body away for autopsy, Odo had hurried Quark to his office, commanding him to stay or get charged with murder. Quark had stayed while Odo watched the autopsy and spoke with Commander Sisko.

When Odo arrived, Quark was pacing. Small dusty footprints marred Odo's normally clean floor. Quark had apparently been pacing the entire time Odo was gone.

"Commander Sisko wants your game closed down," Odo said.

"What for?" There was just a hint of panic in Quark's voice.

"Well," Odo said slowly, "since it is the scene of a rather interesting murder, I believe he's afraid that another may occur. So until we catch the killer, I will have to shut down the bar."

Quark stood. "You can't do that! I need it open. At least, the back room. By tomorrow morning. I'm sure that will be possible."

"Really?" Odo smiled. "What do you need the room for?"

"Nothing really. Just a few games."

"Nothing? Then you won't mind having the bar closed for, say, a week."

"A week!" Quark stood. "I can't have that!"

"I am investigating a murder, Quark. You were found holding the body."

"I didn't kill anyone."

"So you say."

"The room was dark. Anyone could have come in or left."

"The computer records say that only Rom used the door. Are you saying Rom killed the woman?"

"Yes! No! I am not saying anything." Quark slid his chair back, away from Odo.

"Except that you want to have the room available tomorrow morning. For a few games, Quark? Exactly what type of games?"

Quark shifted in his chair. A bead of sweat fell from his chin onto his shirt. "Card games," he said. "Nothing more than a few simple card games. Actually, poker."

"Don't withhold information from me, Quark," Odo said. He leaned toward Quark. "You are holding a poker tournament and you expect to make a great deal of money doing so."

"But how did you . . . ?" Quark let the question drop.

"You can't hide things from me in this station." It had been a fairly simple deduction. He had never seen so many formal looking tables in Quark's back room. That, plus the information Odo had received on the visitors landing at the station, combined with the news of L'sthwan, made Quark's plan very clear.

The handful of players Odo had spoken to after the murder had confirmed it: Quark was planning one of the biggest poker tournaments the quadrant had ever seen.

But Quark hadn't counted on L'sthwan. Identifying him among all the players might take some effort.

"The tournament will be quite entertaining," Quark said. "You should drop by and watch some of the action."

"Assuming," Odo said, "that I allow the card tournament to go on."

"No! You couldn't. I've been planning this for years. Some of the best players in the sector are here."

"There is the little matter," Odo said, "of the murder."

"I'm sure," Quark said, "that with your great detective skills you will soon have the guilty party in custody."

"I may already have the guilty party in custody."

"I did not kill her!"

"No," Odo said. "You merely moved her body."

Quark looked down. "I was bringing her to you."

"You were going to hide her until the tournament was over."

"It wouldn't have made any difference!"

Some days Odo wished that Quark had vanished with the Cardassians. If that had happened Odo's job would have been a lot easier, if less interesting. "Of course not," Odo said, letting the sarcasm control his tone. "It would only give the murderer time to escape."

"He may already have done that."

"So you said." Odo leaned on his desk and crossed his arms in front of his chest. "If you are as innocent as you claim, that means the murderer was in the room when the lights went out."

"People were using the door."

"*Rom* used the door, at your insistence. I got that much of the story from the handful of people I spoke with. I do not believe that someone would wait for accidental darkness, then slip into a room he had never seen before to murder a specific person. No, the murderer was there."

Quark frowned. "What's your point?"

"My point is this," Odo said slowly. His skin tingled. He would enjoy Quark's response to this suggestion. "When the tournament starts tomorrow morning, I need to have a seat at one of the tables."

"You can't play poker! You won't understand a thing." Quark stood, as if that settled the matter.

"You have been encouraging me for a long time to learn to gamble," Odo said, walking to Quark's side and looking down on him.

Quark's body trembled. The sweat dripped off his ears. "You need one hundred bars of gold-pressed latinum to enter."

"No, I don't," Odo said. He graced Quark with a rare half-smile. "You need to make money off this game, and as host, you can't play yourself. The house take would never satisfy a Ferengi. Am I right, Quark?"

"I will make a good profit on this game," Quark said.

"Yes." Odo blocked Quark's path to the door. The sharp fermented scent of Ferengi sweat had grown stronger. "You will make a profit by putting your own players in the game. I suspect they will not always play by the rules."

"Everyone has to play by the rules."

Odo tilted his head. "Don't lie to me, Quark. I can shut your tournament down in an instant."

Quark's chin jutted out. "If I let you play, will you keep the bar open?"

"Yes," Odo said. He resisted the urge to rub his hands together. Quark was finally beginning to understand.

"I only have room for eighty players," Quark said,

"and there was already someone waiting to take the dead woman's place."

"Get rid of one of your players," Odo said. "I will take his place."

"You can't be a ringer if you can't play cards."

"You want to make a profit," Odo said, "and I want to catch a murderer. It seems to me, Quark, you had better teach me how to play poker."

"By tomorrow morning?"

"Unless you want to postpone your game."

Quark gritted his teeth. "You'd better be a quick learner, Constable, because if you aren't, those other players will eat you alive."

"I believe that's your problem," Odo said.

CHAPTER
7

JAKE SISKO tried to look relaxed as he walked through the Promenade. But the emptiness of the Promenade bothered him. So did Nog's insistence that everything would be all right.

The last time Nog had told Jake that, Jake's father had grounded him for a week. Jake didn't want that to happen again.

And it would if his father caught him. His father had clear rules: when there were problems in the station, Jake was supposed to return to their quarters. The flickering lights, the awful earthquakelike shaking, and the blackouts meant trouble.

Jake had tried to stay in his quarters. He had contacted Nog and asked him to come over for some cake. But Nog didn't like cake—at least, not chocolate cake. He always complained that it didn't crunch and that it had been dead far too long to taste good.

Instead, Nog had suggested that Jake meet him in the Promenade.

Jake had said no. But when his father notified him that the problems would keep him away for hours, Jake got bored. He contacted Nog and asked what was happening in the Promenade. Nog wouldn't say, but he had promised that it would be great. This time Jake paused only for a moment. All he could do in his quarters would be to pace while he worried if his dad was all right.

Being busy was better.

Nog moved with a typical Ferengi scuttle that somehow seemed faster than regular human pace. Jake had to hurry after him. He was afraid the lights would go out again and the smoke in the corridor made him uneasy.

"Nog," he said, "I think maybe we should go to my quarters. I have an old-fashioned chess set that my father brought from Earth."

"Flat board?" Nog asked.

Jake nodded. He had been wanting to try it since he had first seen it.

"No challenge in it. And besides, you won't bet."

"You don't bet on chess."

"My father does," Nog said.

Jake sighed. Nog's father bet on everything. Nog didn't seem to understand games played without wagers. "Where are we going?"

"Just wait. You'll love it."

Nog had said that about sautéed grub beetles too. Jake couldn't eat food that still moved. Still, he followed Nog toward Quark's. They took the stairs leading to the second level of the Promenade. Their boots rang against the metal. The sound sent a shiver down Jake's back. Usually the Promenade was so noisy that he couldn't hear himself think, let alone walk.

When they reached the top Nog led him to the solid glass wall that looked down into Quark's. No one sat in the bar. The Dabo girl leaned over her table looking bored.

"No one's in there," Jake said. "I think we should go to my quarters."

But Nog wasn't paying attention. He was using a small laser driver to take off a panel on the wall. Quietly, he set the panel on the floor, then looked around. Jake looked too. They were alone.

Nog crawled into the hole. "Come on," he said, his voice echoing.

Jake's heart pounded in his throat. His father had better be busy in Ops. Jake could get grounded for more than a week for this. His dad had given him strict instructions to stay out of the service areas of the station. They were just too dangerous. But it seemed that standing out in the hall arguing with Nog would cause more problems. So he ducked inside.

The service walkway was hot and lit with tiny lights on each side of the flooring. Probably emergency lighting. If everything shut off now, he and Nog would be in deep trouble.

Nog reached around him and refastened the panel.

"This better be worth it," Jake said.

Nog raised a finger to his lips. "It is," he whispered.

A bead of sweat ran down Jake's face. The service walkway they crouched on extended toward Quark's. When it reached the bar, it became a catwalk, supported by cables. It did look interesting. "Where does this go?"

"Holosuites on both sides," Nog said, pointing. "Follow me."

Jake stared at the wall where the suites were. He really didn't want to see what happened in those suites. His dad had explained the facts of life to him years ago, but what his dad described and what happened in the holosuites didn't sound like the same thing at all. Just the thought of some of the stuff he had heard made his stomach twist.

Bent over in almost an apelike crouch, Nog led the way down the service walkway between huge cables, blank walls, and support beams. Jake followed, his damp palms sliding on the metal. Something pierced his thumb, and he stifled a cry. Nog looked up at him with a frown and put a finger to his lips again. Jake paused, wiped his hands on his pants, and continued his descent.

Suddenly Nog turned to the right and followed an even thinner path over what looked to be the ceiling of a room. Jake could hear talking and laughing from below.

". . . really matter," a male voice said. "Just gets rid of some of the competition."

"Well," a woman replied. "I'm not sure I want to play with the kind of riffraff who believe in killing the opponent."

"Never played poker, have you, lady?"

The voices made Jake freeze. They had a harsh sound that he didn't like. Nog stopped and pointed.

At first Jake couldn't figure out what it was he was supposed to see. Ceiling tiles, support joists, and the backs of light fixtures stuck through the tiles. He inched closer. The voices became a blur.

"I saw my dad and Quark in here last week," Nog whispered. "They were laughing about how much this would make them when the tournament started."

Tournament? Poker? Quark was up to something, and Nog knew about it. Jake examined the area Nog was pointing to. Attached to the back of a normal, small light fixture was a sophisticated sensor system. "What's it for?"

Nog punched his shoulder. "Look, there are a bunch of them. One over every table."

"Why?"

Nog looked at him as if he were an idiot, so Jake studied the sensors spaced throughout the ceiling. From what he could remember from the unit Chief O'Brien did at school, these sensors would be able to not only record visual data and sound, but all medical data of any person they were pointed at.

Laughter resounded below. Jake jerked back, startled. Nog put a hand on his shoulder.

"There's going to be a big card tournament," Nog whispered. "Come here." He led Jake over to a small hole in the ceiling where a tile had slipped slightly, letting a sliver of light into the darker service area. "Look through there."

Jake did as he was told. Below, the room was brightly lit. The table had a green felt surface, piled with chips and cards. From his vantage point, he could make out the legs of one man sitting in a chair. In the man's hand were cards.

"Your dad's cheating?" Jake asked, turning back to Nog. "He can see every hand of cards."

Nog laughed quietly. "Yeah, isn't it great? With those sensors he can see every detail in the place *and* judge someone's emotional state. I just wish I knew where it was being broadcast to. Wouldn't you just love to watch the monitors?"

Jake just crouched there looking at his friend. No, he thought, actually, he wouldn't.

CHAPTER
8

"MAKE THIS FAST, QUARK," Odo said. "I have a murder investigation to conduct."

Quark took a kerchief out of the pocket of his sweater and wiped his brow. The environmental controls were still out, and Odo's office was hotter than ever. They couldn't leave the door open because Quark didn't want anyone to know what they were doing.

With a sweep of his arm, he pushed aside everything on Odo's desk. Odo moved quickly to catch files before they fell to the floor. Odo's deep frown made Quark feel a little better, anyway. Although nothing could make him feel good. The murder had only added to the complications. Quark had another worry he hadn't even discussed with anyone.

The Grand Nagus.

If the tournament succeeded, the Nagus might want

to buy the bar. He had hinted as much the last time he visited Deep Space Nine. If the tournament did not go well, Quark would be embarrassed in front of the Nagus.

And then there was the matter of the entrance fee. All of the Nagus's money was supposedly destroyed with his ship. He asked Quark to front him the entrance fee. Quark could hardly say no.

He didn't want to think about what would happen if the Nagus lost. The Nagus never paid his gambling debts.

"I hope you had a purpose in clearing my desk," Odo said.

Quark reached into his other pocket and pulled out a regular deck of cards. He slapped it on the desk's surface. "Sit down. I'm going to teach you to be the best player in the quadrant."

"I don't want to be the best," Odo said. "And I have already learned how to play."

Quark leaned forward, hand still cupping the deck. "Every single player here is the best in the quadrant. The only way you'll survive long enough to play more than one round is by being one of the best yourself. Now, I'm going to start with the basics."

Odo sighed, sat down, and leaned forward. "Not too basic. I have already looked up poker in the computer. It's quite simple."

"Simple?" Quark sat down. The heat made it hard to breathe. "You have never gambled and you think poker is simple?"

"It seems quite logical to me."

"Don't you understand, Odo? These are the best poker players in the known universe. We can't put you up against them."

"We will, or I will shut the game down," Odo said. His half-finished features looked calm.

Quark wanted to strangle him. Odo could be calm, of course. His life wasn't on the line. The Grand Nagus wasn't threatening his profit. No, all he had to do was be a ringer and he wasn't going to be very good at that.

"I understand the rules," Odo said.

"No, you don't," Quark replied. "Do you know what a bluff is?"

"When a player pretends he has a better hand than he does." Odo leaned back. "I don't know if I can do that."

"It's the essence of poker! You have to bluff! *Everyone* bluffs!" Quark knew he was shouting, but he couldn't stop.

"I prefer to be direct," Odo said.

Quark buried his face in his hands. Odo would get caught and Quark would be the laughingstock of the gambling world. He would never hold another tournament again. All that money . . .

"Quark, I have an investigation so I need to cut—"

Quark brought his head up. No use fighting it. These were the cards he was dealt. He took a deep breath. "Poker has several variations. We are going to play Seven Card Hold'Em."

Odo held up his hand to stop Quark. "I learned the game from the computer. There is no need to waste my time and—"

"We are going to waste your time," Quark said, barely controlling his temper, "if we are wasting my money with this stupid idea. Now let me continue."

Odo nodded and Quark went on. "Seven Card Hold'Em means that seven cards are dealt and the best five cards win. That's the basis of the game. Nothing more. You understand that?"

Odo shrugged. "It sounds like all the other seven-card poker games I read about."

"It's not," Quark said. "This one requires a lot more skill. And remember, poker is skill."

"It's all chance. You can't control the cards you're dealt. Unless your dealers will make sure that—"

"That's childish cheating!" This heat was impossible. Quark stood up and began pacing. "Poker is a game of skill. The skill comes in the bluff. Anyone can win with a bad hand if that person bluffs well and never has to show his cards. Do you understand?"

"I understand that bluffing is very important to you." Odo folded his hands on the desk. "Now, would you please finish?"

Quark shuffled the deck and sighed. "I'm sure it won't make a difference."

"Excuse me?" Odo said.

Quark ignored him and dealt two cards to Odo and himself. "The dealer will give you two cards facedown like this. Don't show them to anyone else, no matter what. After you get those two cards there is a round of betting."

Odo picked up his cards.

"Betting is the essence of poker."

"I thought bluffing was," Odo said.

"If you didn't bet, you would have no reason to bluff." Quark sat down. He should have been checking on his surveillance system. He should have been mingling with his guests. He should *not* have been teaching this unfinished, serious-minded security officer how to play a game.

"I don't think I like this game," Odo said. "It seems far too easy."

"You don't have to like it. You just have to play it."

Odo sighed. "All right. Please finish."

Quark refrained, but just barely, from tossing the entire deck at Odo. After a few more deep breaths, he dealt three cards faceup. A queen of hearts, a six of spades, and a deuce of spades. Nice. With the king and five of spades in his hand, he had a nice flush going. Too bad he wasn't really playing. "After the betting has stopped," he said, "the dealer will put the next three cards in the center of the table, faceup. That is called the Flop."

"Why?" Odo asked again, staring at the cards Quark had placed faceup between them.

"Because it creates flop sweat," Quark lied. He wiped his face again. "Don't ask what flop sweat is."

"I'm not sure I want to know." Odo turned a card upside down in his hand. He moved his hand close to the three cards in front of him.

"Don't do that!" Quark said. "You don't want anyone to see in your hand."

"You mean they'll look?"

"Let me explain this to you again." Quark set his cards and the deck down. "Poker is a game of skill for liars and cheats. It is a great way to make a lot of money on the strength of a single lie. Most tournaments are set up so that no one cheats. But there is no rule against peeking into another player's hand. Nor is there a rule against getting a player to blurt out his hand. If someone suspects that you are a novice, they'll tell you all sorts of lies. If you have any questions, you ask me. Is that clear?"

"Very clear," Odo said. "In fact, clearer than it has

ever been. I can handle cheats and liars." He pulled his cards closer to his chest, but not before Quark saw the three and four of spades. If only he had that knowledge in a real game. If only Odo were a true player who would bet on a possible straight flush, the best hand there was.

Quark shook his head. It would be a long night. "Another round of betting goes on after the Flop," he said, letting his exhaustion and disappointment creep into his voice. "Then the dealer places a fourth card faceup on the table." Quark did so. It was the five of spades.

Oh, perfect hand. Quark had just dealt to Odo the inside card of a straight flush. With the knowledge he had and that hand he would have destroyed anyone in a regular game. But this wasn't a regular game. And Odo had the hand.

"Then there is a final round of betting," Quark said. "And finally the dealer places the fifth and last card on the table and there is one more round of betting."

Quark turned up the final card. The queen of diamonds. What an interesting group of cards. It would have made for great play in the tournament.

Odo nodded, studying the two cards in his hand and the five on the table. Quark was certain that Odo had no idea what he was looking at.

"You make the best hand you can using the two cards in your hand and any three cards on the table. When the betting is done with the last round, you have what is called the Showdown."

"The Showdown?"

"An accurate term," Quark said. "The person who made the last raise in the bet must place his cards faceup on the table to show his hand. If another player thinks he has a better hand, he must then show it also. The best hand takes all the bets."

Odo nodded, still staring at the cards. "I think I understand. It is a very simple game."

Quark half snorted, then said, "I'm sure you do understand."

Odo glanced up at him with a slight smile. "I understand it's your money I'm playing with."

That thought almost sent Quark into tears, but he choked them back. He stood to leave, but then another thought occurred to him. "That security uniform of yours might make some of my guests a little nervous," Quark said to Odo. "Could you wear some other clothes?" Quark realized he had never seen Odo in anything but his brown Bajoran garb. "Do you *own* any other clothes?"

"Don't be stupid," Odo said, and leaned forward as his brown uniform turned a molten red, then reformed into a blue and orange civilian jumpsuit. "I don't own *any* clothes."

CHAPTER
9

THE LIGHTS FLICKERED AGAIN.

"Hang on," Sisko said and reached for the edge of the communications board in front of him. All of Ops shook, but the officers stayed at their stations. They had become used to the rumblings.

Sisko wiped his face with the back of his hand. He didn't know what it was about Cardassian engineering that meant that places grew stifling hot when the environmental controls went down.

O'Brien crouched over the engineering station, his hands shaking. About four A.M. he had grabbed a moment and fixed the replicators. Now he was on what must have been his tenth cup of coffee—the old-fashioned kind. With caffeine. Without looking up O'Brien said, "We lost a few of the lifts that time and power is out in two of the docking bays. A light one compared to the last few."

A light one. They were all getting used to this. Sisko

remembered a friend who had spent a decade in Tokyo once saying that people who lived in earthquake country never relied on the ground. He was beginning to understand that. "Dax, what have you got?"

Dax hadn't moved from the science station all night. Even though her posture remained erect, the shadows under her eyes made them look black and blue. She had been coming off a shift when this started. "It's the same, Benjamin. I'm not getting anything except those subspace fluctuations. They run across a number of bands, but randomly. I can't pinpoint any direct cause."

"Neither can I," said Carter, the slender woman who had arrived at two A.M. to take Dax's place. The relief crew had shown up, but the original crew had not left.

All of his officers were showing the strain of the odd events. Sisko moved to the station beside communications. He had punched the same diagnostic every hour hoping for a change. Still no external evidence of damage. No external cause. It was as if the station were experiencing its own earthquake—as if something from inside were causing the rumblings and the power fluctuations.

But that didn't feel right to him, especially since the Cardassians had experienced the same phenomenon. Those subspace fluctuations were a clue. Something that the crew couldn't see, something that their sensors could barely detect, was harming the station. Sisko wanted it to end.

Now.

"Commander," O'Brien said, "the breakdowns seem to have different sources. This time the lifts were shut down by power surges that tripped safety systems. But the power in the docking bays went out without any indication of a surge. Under normal circumstances I would say that the two are not even related occurrences."

"But actually they are," Sisko said. The puzzle was getting more confounding.

O'Brien glared at his board. "Finding the connection is the problem." O'Brien stifled a long yawn, took another sip of his coffee, and went back to his work.

Sisko went to the replicator and ordered a coffee for himself. Then he changed the order to a double cappuccino. Caffeine that tasted good. Fatigue dripped off him with the sweat. He changed the order again to an iced cappuccino.

"Commander," Kira said. She had taken his place at the communications board. The more tired Kira got, the more she worked like a whirlwind. After long shifts, Sisko had seen her collapse in the turbolift. As a commander, he valued that energy. But he also worried that one day Kira would push too hard. "I have a message from the Bajoran planetary defense."

"On screen," he said. He took the glass out of the replicator and sipped, letting the chill contrast with the ache of his overheated body. Bajoran planetary defense. Without hearing the message, he knew he would be facing another problem.

Kira was peering at him. She had seen his hesitation. "Sir, maybe I should take this one."

"On screen, Major Kira." He would deal with any problem. He had seen Kira's attempts at diplomacy.

"Sir, they're not happy—"

He tilted his head and smiled just a little at her. "Major, I have dealt with angry Bajorans before."

Kira's lips pursed. O'Brien stifled a laugh and Dax grinned. They were all getting punchy. Normally the crew would not have reacted to that statement. Normally, Sisko wouldn't have said it.

He set his cappuccino down on the cup holder beside the nearest work station and walked to the front of the operations table. "On screen, Major."

"Yes, sir," she said.

The screen flickered for a moment, then the head and shoulders of a Bajoran woman appeared. She was about Sisko's age, but the weight of her duties had turned the hair near her temples silver. Her eyes and mouth were heavily lined, making her look as if she had shouldered a heavy burden for a long time. Behind her was a window that overlooked the fountains of Bajor and a wall covered with medals. "Commander Benjamin Sisko?"

"Yes," he said, uncertain to whom he was speaking.

"Captain Litna, Head of Bajoran Planetary Defense. Bajor asked the Federation to provide protection from the Cardassians. You are in charge of providing that protection. You are failing."

Sisko felt the exhaustion run through him. He was no diplomat, and it became harder to be one when he was tired. "The treaty with the Cardassians—"

"The treaty with the Cardassians, whatever it *was*, obviously is no longer, Commander." Litna's lined face moved closer to the screen. "We have been under attack since last night."

"So have we," Sisko said. "But the Cardassians—"

"Good," Litna said. "Since we are suffering the same fate, I trust you will do something about it."

She pushed a button and her face winked off the screen. Sisko almost asked Kira to hail Litna again, but then stopped. If he solved the problem for the station, he would solve it for the Bajorans. Then he would contact Captain Litna and talk with her. Only then.

He hoped that would be soon.

"Great diplomacy, Commander," Kira said. Her hands were clasped behind her back and she stalked him like a cat about to pounce on its prey. "Litna is only the greatest fighter Bajor has ever seen. If we do not take action, she will take matters into her own hands."

Sisko picked up his iced cappuccino and took three long gulps. The bitterness of the coffee reminded him that he had not ordered sugar, but no matter. The coolness soothed his throat. Maybe Kira was right. Maybe he should soothe the captain's feelings. "Contact her again, Major," Sisko said. "Tell her the Cardassians are not at fault. And tell her that we are working on the problem."

"I could have done that in the first place," Kira said. Sisko leveled a gaze at her and she had the grace to flush. "Sir."

She returned to her place at the communications station. Sisko bent over the operations table. Too many lights blinked, revealing the outages all over the station.

"Excuse me, Benjamin," Dax said. "The fact that Bajor is involved brings a whole new dimension to this situation. We haven't eliminated any possibilities. For all we know the Cardassians may well be involved."

Sisko stood and rubbed his back. The odd stress had turned into aches all over his body. "They contacted us, Dax, about their ships. I think that something else is going on."

O'Brien snorted. "Or maybe that was a ruse. I wouldn't put it past them." The hatred in his voice was obvious.

Sisko turned and glared at him, but O'Brien never looked up from what he was working on.

"Commander," Kira said, "Captain Litna is not responding to my signal."

"Bajoran women," O'Brien muttered.

Sisko ignored him. "When you do reach her, reassure her that we are doing everything we can to determine what is going on. Try to calm her about the Cardassians so that she doesn't do anything rash."

"Yes, sir." Kira's hands flew across the communications board.

"Brace yourselves," Dax said suddenly.

Sisko grabbed the edge of the operations table as the lights flickered. He waited for the accompanying bumps, but none came.

"Power down in the heating systems," Carter said.

"Communication knocked out," Kira said.

"A small one again," Dax said. "No other damage."

"Except . . ." O'Brien's pause sounded ominous.

Sisko let go of the operations table with reluctance. The heat in the room seemed to have gone up, although he knew it couldn't have. He looked up. O'Brien was frowning at the engineering console. "Except, Mr. O'Brien?"

"Well, sir," O'Brien said, "I've been monitoring the power core since I got up here. This last reduced our power level by two percent. Power was already down five percent when I got here."

"What are you telling me, Chief?" Sisko asked.

O'Brien looked up and Sisko saw that all trace of exhaustion had gone from his face. Something else had replaced it. Despair? Frustration? Sisko couldn't tell. "I'm saying, sir, that these fluctuations are affecting the power core. I need to run a few more diagnostics, but based on the evidence, each time the lights flicker, the structural integrity of the core is weakening."

Sisko glanced at the operations table. There was no warning light blinking on the power core, but a small red number indicated that core output was down almost 10 percent. If it went too low, key systems would quit. "How long before we lose life support?"

"I don't know if it will go that far, sir," O'Brien said. "It's just something we have to watch. Actually I'm more concerned that a big hit could knock out the power core containment fields."

Sisko nodded. He didn't have to be told what that meant. If the containment field went down, there would be little left of the station except some hard radiation. "Watch it close, Mr. O'Brien. Keep me posted on any changes." He walked up the steps to the science console. Dax's posture was slipping. He could feel the exhaustion radiate from her. "Dax, you had warning this time. Have you got something?"

"Not really," she said. She gripped the science station with one hand. Her knuckles were white. How many hours had she been on duty? Thirty-six? Forty? "I noticed the subspace fluctuations that we've seen before. In the past, though, they have come after the event. This time, they came before. In fact, there doesn't seem to be any real pattern to them at all."

"Computer, what's causing the subspace fluctuation?"

"There are over twenty subspace fluctuations currently noted," the computer said. "No cause available."

"I tried that already, Benjamin," Dax said. "Computers can't solve everything." The calmness had left her tone. She had actually snapped at him, in a quiet, Dax-sort of way.

"I am aware of that," he said, keeping his voice level. He needed his crew as sharp as possible. "You look tired, Dax. How many shifts have you worked in a row?"

"Three," she said. "I think."

"Ensign Carter, will you relieve Lieutenant Dax? Dax, show Carter those subspace fluctuations."

Dax sat up straighter, as if the threat of being relieved of duty gave her extra energy. "Benjamin, I think I should stay."

"I think you should go, Dax. Rest, and eat. We all will have to take breaks if this continues. Report back in an hour to relieve one of us."

Dax shook her head. "Benjamin—"

He held up a hand to stop her. He knew what she was going to say. She had the most experience with odd phenomena. If they were going to solve the problem scientifically, then chances were she would find the answer. Right now, that argument wasn't good enough.

Sisko smiled at her. "Old man," he said. "You might get some insight if you sleep. Having you rest will benefit all of us. Now go."

She sighed, and as the air left her body, it wilted.

Her face was ashen, the brown patches on her skin standing out in sharp relief. "Yes, sir."

Carter made her way to the science station. Sisko walked over to the engineering station. O'Brien looked tired too, but he hadn't worked as long as Dax.

"Chief," Sisko said, "make sure the power core containment is as solid as you can get it, then focus on the environmental controls. Get those back up as quickly as possible. Kira, you work on the communications until O'Brien is free. And Kira?"

She stopped and looked up at him.

"As soon as you get communications back on-line, get in touch with Starfleet. Explain our situation. Ask if they have any information as to what is going on."

Kira gave him a look that chilled him. She liked to solve things on her own. But if the problems extended from Cardassian space to Bajor, then something big was going on.

He had to find out what it was.

CHAPTER
10

GARAK MOVED the silk lingerie closer to the front door. The lingerie wasn't very valuable, but it did attract the eye. He didn't want his most expensive clothing on display while he was out of the shop. If he had his druthers, he would have put all the clothing in the back and covered the windows. But he didn't have the time or the storage space.

He took the green and gold loose weave cloaks, perfumed with a salty, rainlike scent, and moved them to the back. He had already placed the Tharethian evening gowns into the dressing rooms, and his specialty, the long-waisted, seventh-century-cut Cardassian suit (which could fit any humanoid body form with just a bit of tinkering—and look good on all) behind his desk.

Then he scanned the shop. The paintings added a bit of color, as did the red dressing room curtains. The mirrors reflected the dullest of his creations, left out only so that the passersby would know that a clothier remained on Deep Space Nine.

He smiled. For the next day at least, he would not be a clothier. He would be a gambler. He hadn't played since his comrades left the station. Ferengi and humans rarely played poker with the kind of cutthroat perfection he preferred. He had watched a back room game at Quark's once and decided that it wasn't worth his time. But he had overheard Quark listing some of the luminaries who would attend this tournament and he wanted to test his skill against theirs. He was considered the best Cardassian poker player in the region but had rarely played against others with reputations as good as his.

For months he had thought of this game, going over plays in his mind. He even rented a holosuite (disgusting place) and replaced Quark's program with his own: a series of games against the best poker players in the last two centuries. He had done very well, but somehow playing against three-dimensional imagery lacked the excitement of the real thing.

He grabbed his special CLOSED sign and was about to paste it to the doors when they slid open. Two Klingon women swung in, their long hair flowing down their backs. He had always admired Klingon dress: the strength of armor with the diamond cut between the breasts to suggest femininity. Someday he would do a line of Klingon clothing.

Although he knew these two would never buy. B'Etor and Lursa, renegade Klingons from the House of Duras. They had tried to take over the Klingon High Council a few years back and failed. Since then they had been trying to raise enough money to build a new army. So far nothing had worked.

Obviously, they hadn't realized his part in defeating their last attempt.

"Ladies," he said, bowing slightly at the waist. "I am afraid I am closed today."

Lursa grabbed a silk teddy and crumpled it before tossing it to the ground. "We are not interested in such trifles."

"Really?" Garak said. "I know of no other reason to visit a clothier."

"Do not mock us, Cardassian," B'Etor said.

"I wouldn't dream of it." Garak bowed again. "How may I help you?"

Lursa stalked toward his desk, her slit skirts revealing her muscular legs. He cringed as she pushed aside the rack holding three Cardassian suits. Then she leaned on his desk. He followed, B'Etor behind him.

Perhaps they did know that he had betrayed them to the Federation the last time they were on Deep Space Nine. He had cost them a small fortune in gold-pressed latinum. Women like this carried a grudge.

"We understand," B'Etor said, "that you are playing in the poker tournament."

Garak nodded, not pleased that he had to practice his poker face so early. His day would have gone better if these Klingons had not arrived.

"Your shop must be quite profitable for you to afford the hundred bars of gold-pressed latinum entry," Lursa said.

"I am a clothier, madam," Garak said, allowing his voice to rise just a bit in protest. "Not a simple garment seller."

B'Etor laughed, a hard, cackling sound. "Small people are so easy to offend."

"We have a proposition for you," Lursa said.

"A business proposition," B'Etor added.

"I'm always interested in business." Garak clasped his hands. He would wait them out. Odd that they would come to him after the last deal. But then he was their only contact on the station. Either that or they were going to make him pay for betraying them.

"We thought you might be interested in business." Without the slightest hint of movement a deck of cards appeared in Lursa's hands. She shuffled them twice and then placed them on his desk.

"Smooth," he said. He started to reach for the deck but B'Etor stopped him. Her arm, brushing against his, was cold. For a moment he thought she was going to grab him. Instead she reached forward and cut the cards, then nodded for Lursa to deal.

"This deck," B'Etor said, "assumes six players. We will have decks for five and seven players if the table allows."

Garak's throat was dry. The shop was cool compared to the rest of the station, but with the environmental controls out of order, the air had become stale.

Lursa dealt six hands, two cards each, facedown on the counter. She poked her finger at the hand two to the left of the dealer. "This hand will be the best in the six-player deck. In a five-player deck, the best hand will be the one immediately to the dealer's right. The best hand, in a seven-player deck, will be the one three from the dealer on the right."

Garak nodded when Lursa looked at him. He said nothing, not sure yet what they expected of him.

"All the other hands," B'Etor said, "will be strong to keep the bets high. But we will know the winning hand."

Lursa dealt the three flop cards and then the remaining two up cards. Garak reached across and turned up the winning hand. When the women said nothing, he smiled, knowing something was expected of him. "This is all a very old trick. Even if you think Quark will let you get away with somehow switching decks on the dealer, you'll need me because he won't let both of you play at the same table. Right?"

"The dealers are not your concern," Lursa said.

"We control three of the ten," B'Etor added. "But we do need the help at the table."

Garak watched them. He still didn't know why they had come to him. "I assume I'm the only one you have talked to?"

B'Etor glanced over at Lursa, which answered his question. They had already contacted a number of players and were looking for another. The more players, the better the chance of having one sitting in the right position. This kind of stunt could wipe out three or four innocent players at a table, if done correctly.

Garak picked up a few of the other two card hands and studied them. All of them were good hands. All of them would be worth betting a stake on. But none of them were as good as the winning hand. "What's in it for me?"

"If you use one of these decks and then go all the way, we get twenty percent of the total."

Finally, he was beginning to understand. "Let me see. Eighty players at 100 bars of gold-pressed latinum entry fee. That's 8,000 bars total. Take out Quark's five percent and that leaves 7,600 bars. Twenty percent of that is 1,520 bars. Not bad, even after expenses."

Lursa nodded.

"Well?" B'Etor demanded.

"A generous offer." Garak pretended to consider it. "But I think I will decline."

Both women stepped back. "You Cardassian dog!" Lursa said. "The deal is generous. You win a huge hand and—"

"If I am sitting in the right place," Garak said, "I could win over 5,000 bars of gold-pressed latinum in that one hand, and any other day I would be glad to participate. But when it comes to poker, ladies, I am a gambler, not a cheat. I play by skill and I have a reputation to maintain. If anyone saw us together, they would suspect something, and I cannot afford the suspicion."

"You live under suspicion, you ignorant fool," B'Etor said.

"Of being a Cardassian spy." Garak smiled. "I rather like that. It gives me an air of mystery."

"This is unbelievable," Lursa said. "Only an idiot would say no to such a foolproof plan."

Garak rocked on the balls of his feet. "No plan is foolproof, ladies. I am familiar with this trick. Others may be as well."

"Do you plan to turn us in?" B'Etor asked.

"To whom? Quark? He's a Ferengi. He has probably figured out a way to cheat all on his own. No, I will not turn you in. Nor will I be your victim. In exchange for my silence I would like your word that you will warn me when I am at a table where one of your decks is in play." He gathered the cards on his desk.

Lursa scooped the cards from his grasp, and they disappeared in a quick slight of hand that impressed Garak.

Both women stalked for the door.

"I need your word," Garak said.

Lursa stopped and turned to Garak. "You are as stupid as a Romulan peasant."

Garak only smiled. "Your word."

"You will be alerted," B'Etor said.

Garak bowed slightly to the two women. "Good luck to you, ladies."

The automatic doors slid open, and the women walked out of them without looking back. Garak picked up his CLOSED sign and hung it carefully. He couldn't tell them the most important thing. They wouldn't understand. People who gambled for money were fools. Garak would pay his gold-pressed latinum —and lose all one hundred bars if he had to—to play against those of his own caliber.

The game itself was all that mattered.

CHAPTER
11

BASHIR LEANED AGAINST the wall by the door to Quark's back room and watched the activity. He wore a black tuxedo with tails. The coat fit snugly across his chest and the pants added length to his legs. He had bought the tuxedo during his last year at the Academy, when several students had planned a gambling trip to Risa. The trip had never happened and Bashir had longed for an opportunity to wear proper, elegant gambling attire.

He finally had the chance. All he needed was a beautiful woman on his arm and the image he wanted to present—the suave, romantic rake—would be complete.

Only no one was looking at him. The conversation was at a low roar, making individuals hard to hear. Quark was having a quick last word with his dealers, gesturing and pointing with more nervous energy than usual. The Meepod, still bruised from her encounter the night before, limped into the room. She smelled faintly of rotted flesh, a problem with injured Meepods. He did not envy the person who sat next to her.

Nor did he envy the person who was going to sit near the Grabanster. The round, furry, orange male stood just inside the door, giving the entire area an odor of wet dog.

But the group Bashir found himself watching the most were the Romulans. He had met Darak and Kinsak briefly the night before, and had been struck at their cool response to Naralak's death. This morning they actually laughed twice, although they kept their distance from the Klingons.

A Vulcan walked by, head bowed as if in deep meditation. Bashir did a double take. Yes, definitely a Vulcan. How odd. He had met few Vulcans during his service, but he had studied them and their anatomy quite heavily at the Academy. Vulcans did not belong in a gaming hall.

"There you are, you delicious man!" The voice was warm, throaty, and female. Bashir turned in its direction, then wished he hadn't.

Cynthia Jones stood beside him, her pink gown made of a material so thin it revealed everything. Her perfume carried the thick scent of roses. The scent would have been lovely, if she hadn't marinated in it. She ran her finger along his sleeve. "You disappeared on me last night," she said.

He blushed. He had had no intention of seeing her. She had made overt passes since he met her and her tribble in the docking bay. The tribble was clutched in her left hand, like a purse. It cooed at him. "I—I had medical business."

She wrinkled her nose. "The murder. How ugly. I don't suppose there was anything you could do?"

Bashir shook his head. "She was dead long before I saw her. But I did have to tend the Meepod, and Sergei Davidovich—at separate times."

Cynthia laughed. "They always fight. It's a tradition. They hate each other. It goes back to a simple Five Card Stud game played for credits on a supply ship. The story goes that the Meepod called and Davidovich refused to show his cards." She frowned. "Or did Sergei call and the Meepod refuse—? I forget. It doesn't really matter. The grudge was silly, as most of those grudges are." She tucked her arm in his. "I trust you bear no grudges."

He raised his eyebrows, looking around the room for a way out of the conversation. Only Garak, the Cardassian, noticed. He smiled and nodded. Bashir nodded back. They had become friends of sorts since Bashir had helped Garak stop a Bajoran terrorist from dealing with two infamous Klingon women. Those women had gone into the back hall earlier.

Tensions and countertensions and so few of them had to do with the game.

"No," Bashir said, "no grudges. Yet."

Cynthia laughed again and pressed closer to him. "Shall we go in?"

Relief washed through Bashir. Finally, escape! "I'm afraid I can't," he said. "Quark won't let me in the game."

She put a perfectly manicured finger on his lips. The rose perfume shot up his nostrils, and he had to hold back a sneeze. "I thought you said no one held grudges against you."

"Actually, Quark doesn't believe I'm qualified to play."

Cynthia sighed and took her finger away. "Silly man," she said. "Quark doesn't know an experienced player from a novice. All he knows is the color of gold-pressed latinum."

Bashir smiled and slid his arm out of her grasp. "I guess I will have to speak to him," he said. He put his hand on the small of her back and pushed her into the room. "Get your seat. I'll see what I can do."

She gave him a flirtatious glance over her shoulder, then floated into the room. Or at least, it looked as if she floated. The gown almost hid her tiny feet.

Bashir let out the sneeze he had been holding. The odor of dead roses clung to him. Now he would have to get his tuxedo cleaned.

The Grand Nagus of the Ferengi cackled from his chair in the center of the room. Speaking of tensions. If Bashir had to hear that laugh on a continual basis he would go crazy.

A tall, thin creature with an obsidian face and no visible eyes walked past. Bashir stared at it, trying to compare it to things he had read about in his alien anatomy seminar. But he could think of nothing. He would have to call it up on the computer when he got back to his office.

Quark climbed on one of the chairs and clapped his hands to get everyone's attention. Bashir eased into the room. Quark had refused to give him a chair weeks ago, but that wouldn't stop Bashir from watching—at least until Quark kicked him out.

After the noise had died down, Quark smiled. "The First Annual Deep Space Nine Poker Tournament has begun."

Applause and whistles filled the room. Bashir laughed. Even with the problems on the station and the murder, the atmosphere this morning was light.

"My brother Rom will double-check your name against a list of people who have paid their entrance fee. No pay, no play. I'm sure we all will abide by that rule—that way the winner will receive great profit!"

The cheers doubled. Toward the back of the room something chirruped. The Grand Nagus's laugh covered every sound in the room.

Then the lights flickered. The cheering stopped as if someone had stuffed a rag in each player's mouth. Bashir leaned against the wall, feeling that shiver in his back again. When the lights went out the night before, someone had died.

Besides the other problems at the station, by now everyone knew that the Ferengi ship had been destroyed. Bashir had heard conversation in the Promenade Replimat that suggested that the station was under attack. It certainly was malfunctioning. He had had to shave in his office this morning because the hot water was out in his quarters. He still hadn't had his cup of tea and it seemed that the environmental controls were down. The heat in this back room was noticeable now: when the tournament got underway, the heat would probably become unbearable.

The lights flickered a second time, but did not go out.

Quark waved his hands. Obviously, the power fluctuations made him nervous as well. "You will find your initial seating assignments posted on the wall. Your chips will be given to you at your chair after my brother checks your name against the list. Please count your chips in front of the dealer to make sure the amounts are correct."

"Wouldn't want you cheatin' us on chips, now would we, Quark?" asked a bald man in the back, forming the words around his well-chewed cigar.

Bashir smiled to himself. It was just as he'd imagined: rough-and-ready players, as willing to fight as they were to gamble.

Quark sighed. "I am having you count the chips to make sure the game is aboveboard and fair. We want you to have a good time at this tournament."

"Not to mention you want your five percent," said the silver-haired man at the next table. He did not smile as he spoke.

"Well," Quark said, with a huge, insincere grin, "we do need to make a profit, you know."

"There isn't any point in playing if you can't make a profit."

Bashir turned his head sharply. He recognized that dry, sarcastic voice. Odo. He stood at the door to the left of Bashir and, surprisingly, was out of uniform. When Odo saw Bashir looking at him, he nodded.

Quark saw him too and frowned. "We will be starting shortly, so please get ready. And may the best player win."

Quark climbed off his chair as the noise level in the room rose and most everyone moved to the lists posted on the wall. Quark elbowed his way to the entrance. Rom had just stashed the last of the gold-pressed latinum bars in a side room where, Bashir was certain, they would not stay very long.

"Rom!" Quark hissed.

Rom looked up. "It's all there, Quark."

Bashir doubted that too, but the accurate money count was Quark's problem. He moved closer so that he could hear their conversation.

"Any sign of Riker yet?" Quark asked.

Bashir started. Will Riker? First Officer of the starship *Enterprise?* He hadn't heard that a starship was in the area.

"He's not coming," Rom said. "He sent a message last night, but with all the troubles they're having in Ops, it just got relayed now."

"Not coming!" Quark grabbed Rom's ear. "Are you sure?"

Rom pulled a crumpled piece of paper from his pocket. "I made a copy for you to look at. I thought you wouldn't believe me."

The smell of dry paper and mothballs overwhelmed Bashir. He turned to find the Grand Nagus standing beside him. The Nagus was quite fascinating. Bashir would have loved a chance to investigate the Nagus's oversized ears.

"Did you say someone isn't coming?" the Nagus demanded in his nasal voice.

Quark snatched the paper from Rom and scanned it. "Commander Riker from the Federation starship *Enterprise* was supposed to be a player. He sends his regrets. Something about saving a planet or some such." Quark flapped the paper in the air and then handed it roughly back to Rom.

"A pity," the Nagus said, smiling. "He is known to be one of the best players. We will miss his skill."

The Nagus shuffled out of the room. Quark didn't even seem to notice that his leader had left. Bashir watched as word spread through the room that Riker was not coming. Several players were visibly relieved. Apparently Riker was a good games man.

Not that it surprised Bashir. He had met Riker twice and had found him to be the kind of man who belonged on the frontier. Rugged, handsome, competent, Riker had a way with the ladies, and an adventure-filled Starfleet career. Of course a man like that would be an expert at poker.

"We can't be one player short," Quark said to Rom.

"You could play," Rom said.

"Idiot!" Quark grabbed Rom's ear and shook him. "I'm the host. I can't play."

Bashir ran a hand down his tuxedo to make himself look presentable. Suddenly Quark was not the Ferengi owner of a decrepit bar. He was the ticket for Bashir's entrance in the big game.

"Maybe I could—" Rom started.

"No!" Quark twisted Rom's ear. Rom crumpled to his knees. "You will not play. Nog will not play. The Dabo girl will not play. Now be quiet and let me think!"

Of course, Bashir was rusty. He had been planning an extensive gambling trip in Risa on his vacation ever since Quark had turned him down. But he hadn't really played much since he had come to the station.

Quark let go of Rom's ear and paced. "We can't just pull someone off the Promenade—"

"There's no need to," Bashir said. He moved in front of Quark, and Quark nearly bumped into him. "I would like to play."

"You?!?" Quark looked at Rom and both Ferengi giggled, a sound that rivaled the Grand Nagus's laugh. "You're a doctor, not a gambler! You can't even hold your Evarian beer!"

"But I can play poker."

"'But I can play poker,'" Quark said, imitating Bashir's inflections. "*Anyone* can play poker. My nephew can play poker. He just can't play very well."

"I'm sure I could beat your nephew," Bashir said. "And I'm willing to wager I could beat most anyone in that room."

"I'm sure you can . . ." Quark said, ". . . beat my nephew, that is."

"With a stick!" Rom added.

Then they laughed again, doubling over and slapping their knees. Bashir backed up to stay out of their way. He waited until the laughing eased a bit.

"I am a highly ranked poker player," he said.

"Highly ranked at losing!" Rom said. He cackled so hard that he started to cough. Quark patted him on the back and laughed with him.

"I have the entry fee," Bashir said.

The laughter disappeared from Quark's face as if it had never been there. Quark stood up and approached Bashir. Even though Quark only reached Bashir's chest, Quark suddenly seemed taller and stronger. "You have a hundred bars of gold-pressed latinum? How did a Federation doctor get so rich?"

"It's not an unheard of amount of money, Quark."

"It is when it only pays for an hour's worth of poker."

"I plan to play for longer than an hour," Bashir said.

"You didn't answer me, Doctor. Where did you get that kind of money?"

"Do you always quiz your players on where they came about their entry fee?"

"Most of them don't work for the Federation."

"But you were willing to let Will Riker in."

"Riker is a well-known poker player. It's obvious where he got the money."

Bashir crossed his arms in front of his chest. He was not about to tell Quark the truth: no one on the station knew of Bashir's small inheritance, which he had hoarded since his school days. "I got my money in the same place as Commander Riker."

Quark grinned. "And where's that?"

"I won it," Bashir said. "Playing poker."

Quark jerked back and looked him right in the eye. Bashir did not blink. He would bluff. He was good at bluffing. Quark squinted, as if that made Bashir's duplicity clear.

"I have the entry fee in my office," Bashir said.

Quark's eyes widened. Then he sighed. "Get it. You take Riker's chair. But be back immediately. I won't hold the game very long for you."

"You won't have to hold it at all," Bashir said. "This will only take a moment." He started to hurry out of Quark's before he remembered his manners. "And, Quark. Thank you. This will be a great deal of fun."

"Oh, yeah," Quark said. "I can tell. It's already a barrel of laughs."

CHAPTER
12

JAKE CAUGHT HIS BREATH and leaned against an exposed metal wall in the Promenade. Nog tugged on his sleeve, but Jake shook his head. He needed a moment to think.

He had returned home after midnight the night before, dirty, his clothing covered with oils and stains he couldn't identify. He and Nog had had a bad moment climbing out of the service tunnel when they thought one of Odo's guards was going to catch them, but they had managed to elude him. When Jake had arrived at his quarters he had been willing to tell all to his father, but his father hadn't been there.

His father was still working in Ops on the engineering problems and had left a message that Jake should contact him if he had any questions.

Jake had no questions. Except to wonder why *his* father was never there like other boys' fathers were.

"You coming or not?" Nog asked.

"Yeah." Jake's stomach growled. He wished he had had more for breakfast than that glass of orange juice he had grabbed just before he left.

He opened his eyes. Two Klingon women walked past him, their skirts flying. A Hupyrian servant hurried after them. Two Ferengi walked by, talking excitedly. All of them seemed to ignore the faint odor of smoke still in the air.

"Tell me again what we're doing, Nog," Jake said.

"You're following me," Nog said.

He ran up the steps to the second level of the Promenade, his feet ringing on the metal. Jake followed. Nog pulled a side door that led into the upper level at Quark's and both of them ducked inside.

From a hidden space behind the doorway Nog picked up a device that looked like an old-fashioned tricorder. Only it wasn't. It had Ferengi heads imprinted on the back and multicolored buttons that beeped if Nog touched one wrong.

They went back out into the corridor and Nog stopped in front of the service access port they had crawled through the night before.

"I've already seen this," Jake whispered. This was getting old. What did he care if Quark was cheating? His father would have cared, but his father was too busy to notice. Besides, it wasn't as important as keeping the station running.

Nothing was.

Nog shoved the device in the pocket of his sweater and started to work on the panel leading into the service portal.

"I'm not going back in there," Jake said. "We almost got caught yesterday."

Nog just kept working. "You're not going in. I just need you to stand guard."

"For what?"

Nog handed the device to Jake. "I'm going to get a reading on those sensors over the room."

"Why?" Jake asked. The device was warm. It fit his hand. Most human-made equipment was too big for his hands, even after his last growth spurt.

Nog laughed. "So we can track the signals. It has to be a type of signal that wouldn't interfere with the rest of the operation of the station. So it should be easy to track to its source."

Interfere with the operation of the station? Jake frowned. "What are you talking about?"

"This device." Nog took it from Jake's hand. "It scans the signals the sensors are giving out. Someone has to monitor the sensors that are in that ceiling. They have to be in a separate room."

"You mean those sensors are sending signals all over the station?"

Nog pulled off the hatch and crawled in. "I would wager. And that's what I'm going to find out." He looked at Jake. "Don't just stand there. Close the hatch behind me, but not tight. I'll knock when I get back and you open it when no one is in sight. If there's a problem, lean against it until the problem leaves. Got it?"

"What if we get caught?"

"You're in charge of making sure we don't."

Nog disappeared down the service tunnel. Jake looked around and closed the hatch, leaving it open just a crack. Then he walked over to the railing and looked down.

The Klingon women were leaving Garak's clothing store. They looked angry. Klingons always looked angry. No, fierce. They always looked fierce.

A blond human woman, wearing a very thin gown and carrying a fuzzy creature—a tribble?—was walking into Quark's. Jake ran to the stairs to see if he could get a better look, but the woman was lost in the gathering crowd. The faint scent of roses mingled with the smoke.

He glanced at the portal. No Nog.

Jake hurried back to his post. If Quark was sending signals across the station, using a Ferengi device, could it interrupt regular operations? Maybe he could solve the mystery of the station blackouts and stop the cheating all at once.

And maybe lose a friend.

He sighed. He would have to talk to Nog about it.

Keiko O'Brien walked by, her steps precise and familiar. Jake pushed against the wall. He didn't want her to see him. He glanced at his watch. He had thought, with all the problems, that school would be canceled, but no one had told him that. Obviously he was wrong. The teacher was on her way to class now.

A Vulcan walked around her and disappeared into Quark's. Jake waited until Mrs. O'Brien was out of view before peering over the railing into the bar. It looked empty, yet a lot of beings had disappeared into it just since he started watching.

How many people had Quark invited? How important was this thing, anyway?

Important enough that Quark spent hard-earned money on all the equipment in that ceiling.

The lights flickered. Jake shot a glance at the portal. He would hate to get caught in there if the lights went out. He hoped Nog was okay.

The lights stayed on, and Jake let out his breath in relief.

Odo came out of his office, stopped and talked to two of his assistants before heading into Quark's. If anything was wrong, Odo would find it. Maybe then Jake would be off the hook.

He started pacing in front of the hatch. What was taking Nog so long? They had school. They would get caught. Cheers and applause rose from Quark's— very faint cheers and applause. Something was happening. Come on, Nog.

The lights flickered again and Jake braced himself, but nothing happened. The odd shaking that rocked the station hadn't happened for a while. Jake didn't want it to happen again. He stared at the lights overhead, willing them to stay on.

They did.

And Nog wasn't back yet. Jake couldn't leave Nog there. But he didn't want to go in after him. Who knew what happened inside the service hatch when the lights flickered? What if something blew? What if those sensors sent out some weird signal that hurt Nog?

Just when Jake was about to pull open the hatch and go in himself, he heard three faint knocks. He looked both ways. He was alone on the second level. He pulled the hatch open and Nog rolled out, landing on his feet, and grinning.

"What took you so long?" Jake said.

Nog put a finger in front of his mouth. "The sensors are up and working. Really well too."

"How could you tell?"

Nog patted his pocket. The device stuck out of it. "My uncle must be making a lot of money. That room is packed." Nog pulled the device out of his pocket. Its screen glowed red. "Follow me."

"Where?"

Nog laughed. "I don't know, but we'll find out."

He held the device out in front of him as he walked toward the Promenade railing.

"Someone's going to see that," Jake said.

"Who cares?" Nog said. "They won't know what I'm doing."

Butterflies rose in Jake's stomach. Someone would know. Nog led them down the stairs. He clutched the device closer to his chest.

Jake followed, close at Nog's side. "Where'd you get that thing, anyway?"

"It's my dad's," Nog said. "He uses it sometimes when he's trying to find out what my uncle is doing."

"Wouldn't he want it now?"

"Nope. He's in on this one."

A scruffy group of humans with shaved heads and wearing hand-torn clothing hurried into Quark's. Nog walked away from the bar, ignoring the people he passed. The device started beeping. He shut it off and put it in his pocket.

"Here," he said.

"What?" Jake asked. He looked around. They were standing beside a wall in the Promenade. He didn't see anything out of the ordinary. "Nog, is this a joke? Because if it is, I don't like it. Mrs. O'Brien went by and we're going to be late for school—"

"Sometimes you're no fun at all." Nog frowned. "Besides, it's right here."

97

He put his hand on a door with the Cardassian symbol for supplies on it. Across that Quark had put a sticker that said Quark's in four different languages.

"Those sensors are sending signals here?" Jake asked.

Nog nodded and grinned, obviously glad he had recaptured Jake's interest. "There are screens inside that show all the tables in my uncle's back room. The monitors can see all the cards. They must have another system set up to let my uncle's players know who has got what in their hand."

"That's not fair."

"I know. Isn't it great? They're going to make a lot of money."

Jake sighed. Technology. And all those Ferengi sensors sending signals around. No wonder things were going wrong. "Before we go to school, let's stop in Ops and tell my dad. He'll want to know—"

"About cheating in Quark's? Come on, your dad doesn't want to be bothered. He's got enough to worry about. Besides, I don't want to tell anyone." Nog stopped talking as two members of the crew walked by, deep in conversation.

Jake watched them. He didn't recognize either of them. Both ensigns, both wearing engineering colors. Everyone seemed preoccupied this morning. "We've got to tell somebody," Jake said when they passed.

"No, we don't," Nog said. He leaned close to Jake so that Jake could hear him. "My uncle always says information is power. Now we have information on my uncle. We just have to figure out how to use it." He cackled. "Come on. Let's go to school."

Jake glanced at the door. A thin light did come from underneath it. He hated it when Nog got like this. Maybe his dad was right. Maybe there were fundamental differences between Ferengi and humans.

Or maybe not.

CHAPTER
13

ODO WALKED INTO QUARK'S. Already the sound was deafening. Conversation rumbled from the back room. The bar was hot too. The environmental controls were probably out here as well as in Odo's office.

He sighed. He did not want to be here. The game that Quark and the computer had taught him the night before was boring and simple, and Odo didn't understand the attraction in wagering large amounts of money on things that had a great probability of not happening.

Rom was sitting at a table near the door, talking with the Bajoran, Pera. Pera was an interesting case. Odo had spent quite a bit of time studying his file. Pera had had a legitimate job with the Bajoran Provisional Government for one month. Then he had walked away, claiming that the government did not serve Bajoran interests. His background prior to that incident had been an intermittent commitment with the Bajoran Freedom Fighters. Pera would disappear for months, often returning after a Cardassian leader died in a spectacular manner. The Bajoran files were sketchy. The Cardassian files claimed Pera had worked for every terrorist group in Bajor. One of those groups was tied to the Romulans, and the last intermediary the group had used had been Naralak.

Naralak's murder would explain Pera's presence here. Most terrorists didn't have time for poker matches.

"Are you going to stare at us or get your chips?" Rom asked.

Odo picked up his chips as he noted the arrivals with the corner of his eye. A Vulcan he had never seen before. Cynthia Jones, flirting with Dr. Bashir. Xator and Grouk, the Klingons, who were still his primary suspects. Garak. Lursa and B'Etor. More Klingons. Any one of them could be the mysterious L'sthwan.

"Don't you want to count them?" Rom asked.

Odo shook his head. "It's not my money. Why should I?"

He turned and found himself face-to-face with the tall, skinny human from the past. Berlinghoff Rasmussen had a history of cons, with much time spent on Federation penal colonies, but no history of murder. "Not your money?" Rasmussen asked.

"Quark has asked me to sit in on the game," Odo said, "to make sure all of your worthless lives continue long enough for him to make a profit."

Rasmussen frowned. "Doesn't seem like Quark's profit would be of interest to you."

"It's not," Odo said. "But keeping my eye on this collection of thieves and murderers is. There is a lot of

101

money here, Mr. Rasmussen. I will be watching your hands very closely."

"I always keep my cards close to the chest," Rasmussen said.

"I was referring to your real hands. I couldn't care less what you do with your cards." Odo nodded to Rasmussen, and then went into the room.

He glanced at his name on the chart, just as Quark had told him to do. Odo would be sitting close to the door. Good thinking, Quark. The better to observe what was going on.

Right now the other players were looking at their seat assignments and finding their places to sit. Odo sighed. It was time to get to business. He had already been in and out of the room several times, trying to find another way to deal with the murder. He still couldn't come up with a better plan. Perhaps it was fortunate that the game was so easy. It would give him more time to concentrate on the other players.

A familiar laugh from the back of the room made Odo stop. Doctor Bashir was talking with a Vulcan. Both had chips in front of them. Dr. Bashir looked out of place in a black tux. His eyes were wide and his cheeks were flushed, as if he had spent a few hours alone in the holosuite. Odo recognized the look. Bashir wanted to be a part of all of this.

Odo hurried across the room, not caring who he bumped. The Irits, whose name he could not pronounce, nearly dropped its chips. He did not stop to help.

He tapped Doctor Bashir on the shoulder. "Doctor, a word please?"

"Odo!" Bashir said, the pleasure evident in his voice. Really, the boy was too naive. Quark must have seen the entry fee and nothing else. "Are you planning to play?"

"Yes, but I would like to speak with you beforehand."

"It's really not done," Bashir said.

"About the murder," Odo said, keeping his voice level. "Let's go to the Promenade."

"I am not going to leave my chips," Doctor Bashir said. He touched the Vulcan's arm. "No offense meant."

"None taken," the Vulcan said. "The crowd here is disreputable."

"Quite," Bashir said.

Odo rolled his eyes. He was glad he wasn't sitting at this table. The dullest conversationalists of the bunch. "Please, Doctor."

Bashir stacked his chips and stood. He led Odo a few feet away from the table, all the time studying the chips. "I have no other news to give you," Bashir said softly. "The lab reports showed nothing out of the ordinary. The fibers match others we found in the room, and Quark's sweater, of course. The DNA scan revealed nothing. We can only be certain that she died of the knife wound, and death was very quick. Whoever killed her had a knowledge of Romulan anatomy."

"Klingon?"

"I doubt it," Bashir said. "Klingons have honor. They don't usually stab someone in the dark."

"Another Romulan?"

"Possible," Bashir said. "But why here? Why now? And why use a Ferengi knife? I ran some tests on that knife before giving it to your people. It was clean in all ways, except for a bit of chilled grub worm that got into the wound itself. That would suggest to me that the killer had taken the knife from a dinner table and then used it later. There were no prints on the handle."

"Yes, we found that too," Odo said. "Bits of chilled grub worm in the wound. You didn't tell me that before."

"That was the unidentifiable substance I had mentioned last night. It's in my report. I don't suppose you had time to read it."

"Not hardly." Odo had spent too much time with Quark, learning this silly game, and interviewing what suspects he had. Then he spent even more time going over the site with every bit of equipment he had. The oddest thing, and the one he had told no one about, were the strange signals he got, as if someone were monitoring the room. Because of the engineering troubles on the station, he wasn't sure his readings were accurate. He would double-check them later.

The Vulcan brushed Bashir's chips. Bashir took a step forward, then stopped when he realized that the chip piles were undisturbed. "Is that all, Odo? I really must get back."

"No," Odo said. "I want you to keep an eye out for anything unusual. I don't like having a killer loose on my station."

Bashir smiled at him. Odo took a step back. He had not expected that response.

"Knowing gamblers," Bashir said, "I would be surprised if there was *only* one."

CHAPTER
14

THE WALK WAS much too far. The Grand Nagus Zek leaned on his staff and moved as quickly as his wobbly legs would carry him. He had been winded when they reached the turbolift, but now that they were in a hallway leading to the living quarters, he was just plain tired. Still, he could make the walk there and back alone. He was old, but he was not weak. It would do Krax well to remember that.

Krax took the Nagus's arm, but the Nagus shook his son off. Maihar'du, his servant, followed at a close distance, ever ready to assist the Nagus or defend him.

"This is much too far!" the Nagus said. "The game will start without me."

"Quark would not dare start without you," Krax said.

If the Nagus wasn't in such a hurry, he would have boxed Krax's ears. "Quark will do whatever he can," the Nagus said. "He was not too happy about fronting me money to play in the game."

"Especially since we managed to save most of our gold-pressed latinum." Krax giggled. "You are brilliant, Father."

"You should have realized that by now," the Nagus said. "Will the equipment work this far away?"

"Trust me, Father. The setup is perfect."

The Nagus cackled. "Trust you? I'm not that old. Now quit babbling and show me."

"We should have come earlier this morning, Father, when we had time."

The Nagus gripped his staff tighter. One more comment like that and he would box Krax's ears with the staff, here, in the corridor. "I want to see how it works when there are people in the room. You cannot leave these things to chance, Krax."

"Yes, Father," Krax said.

He stopped in front of a door that looked like any other through the ring. He pressed the lock on the side and the door slid open, revealing a Ferengi screen made of black cloth and decorated with Ferengi heads that matched the one on the staff. The heads were sewn in gold thread.

The Nagus glanced at Maihar'du. His tall, thin humanoid servant had no trouble looking over the screen. "Good work, Krax," the Nagus said. "You have only prevented Ferengi from seeing inside."

Krax was looking at Maihar'du in dismay. "I will fix that, Father."

"See that you do," the Nagus said. He pushed around the screen. The main room of the living quarters was oblong with a large eye-shaped window that opened to the stars. It was not as nice as the one he had stolen from Quark—Quark's quarters this visit, not Rom's—but it still fit ten Ferengi comfortably.

Each Ferengi worked on a makeshift table, staring at small monitors before them. Headsets were pinched to their right lobes and a small implanted microphone behind a gauze privacy screen covered their mouths. The old-fashioned technology worked better in an operation like this, so that the many voices speaking in a room were filtered out. The recipient heard only the voice he was supposed to hear.

The Nagus walked around the first table. The monitor was small—Krax must have borrowed Federation equipment—but it worked. He could see the layout of the first table in Quark's back room perfectly —the green felt surface, the chips littering each place, and the arms and hands of the players. Those who had fingers were playing with chips or tapping nervously on the table's edge. The dealer had placed an unopened deck of cards in front of her place. Each ridge of the design on the back of the deck was visible. Each whirl of ink. Even if the players turned the cards at an angle and held them to their chest, the sensor up above would be able to read them.

"Very good," the Nagus said. "I am glad that Quark has fronted our place in the game because this setup looks like it has cost a small fortune."

"Oh, no, Father," Krax said. "These are your loyal servants who expect only a paltry remuneration for their services. One of the Federation officers donated the monitors when I so kindly asked, and the commander has provided this place out of courtesy for me because our ship was destroyed."

The Nagus smiled. Krax was learning his craft after all. Very good, getting this much equipment at so little cost.

He moved to the second monitor. It too showed a table covered with chips. No game had started yet. He was right. Quark would wait.

"Quark does not know of this?" the Nagus asked.

"He was not around when we tracked his signals. We found his sensor devices late last night. They are in perfect position. We can bleed the information off of them with no problem." Krax stood at his full height when he spoke, as if tracking the signals were his own idea.

"It's a good thing that I knew he would cheat," the Nagus said, using his tone to keep his son in place.

"Yes. Yes, it is, Father. I would never have thought of that myself."

The Nagus pushed Krax. Krax had to catch himself on the back of a chair before he crashed into a third monitor. "That's right," the Nagus said. "You are still too stupid to come up with anything so creative on your own. Now, are our players in place?"

Krax rubbed his shoulder, obviously in pain. Good. Krax had to find a balance between fawning and idiocy. He pointed to four different screens. "We have one at each of those tables. The players all have a receiver just inside the lobe so that we can communicate with them."

"You had them put the receiver well inside the ear, didn't you?" the Nagus asked.

Krax nodded. "Yes, Father. No one has forgotten that unfortunate occurrence on Risa when Gral was caught cheating because the hu-mon next to him overheard the receiver."

"Good," the Nagus said. Krax had gotten the hint. Krax had been the one to improperly place the receivers in that infamous Risa game. The Nagus wanted Krax to make sure the Nagus had not forgotten. Krax could not afford many mistakes. Ever since Krax had blown his chance to become Grand Nagus the last time they had visited this space station, the Nagus had been looking at all of his son's actions with disfavor.

The Nagus grabbed the shoulder of the nearest Ferengi. He did not want to ask Krax this next question. "You have been watching the monitor all morning," the Nagus said. "How has the system been working?"

Krax slid his face between the Nagus and the other Ferengi before the Ferengi had a chance to answer. "Actually, Father, there have been a few bugs."

"A few bugs?" the Nagus said, his voice rising. He should have known better than to trust Krax with a makeshift system. This trip had been a disaster even before the ship blew up. But if they had kept their ship, they would have kept their own equipment and the Nagus would have had more control.

"Nothing serious," Krax said, bowing as he spoke. The Nagus always thought of it as ducking and weaving to avoid a twisting grip on the ears. "I mean, nothing more than the rest of the station is suffering."

"The monitors cut out occasionally," the other Ferengi said, obviously not wanting to be deprived of a chance to speak to the Grand Nagus.

"Cut out? You mean like the lights?"

"Yes, Father." Krax swallowed. The sound was

audible. "You see, it is not too serious. The signals get interrupted, but only when the rest of the station is having problems as well."

"You fool!" the Nagus said. "That could be the most important moment of the game! I am surrounded by idiots who don't even understand the importance of acquisition!"

"Quark will be having the same problem," Krax said, ducking and weaving.

"I do not care about Quark!" The Nagus had had enough. He took Maihar'du's arm and leaned on the staff. "Just make sure the system works. *All of the time.* Do you understand me, Krax?"

"Yes," Krax said, nodding his head so fast it looked as if it would fall off his short little neck.

"If I lose one bar of gold-pressed latinum, just one, due to your idiocy, you will no longer be by my side. Is that clear?"

"Yes, Father," Krax said. "It will work."

At that moment, the lights flickered and every monitor in the place went dark. Ferengi fingers moved across keypads, made fists, and pounded the top of the Federation's screens. One by one, the monitors came back on.

"It will work, eh, Krax?" the Nagus said. He shook his head. Good thing he was playing with Quark's money himself. Then at least the Nagus would make a slight profit—the enjoyment of the game itself—even if Krax's system was a bust.

"Remember," he said, shaking his staff at Krax and the other ten Ferengi. "Every one of you will no longer get special favors and deals from me if this plan fails. Fix those monitors. Now. And Maihar'du?"

The servant nodded.

"Get me back to the game as fast as you can. If that Quark starts without me, I may have to fine him a few bars of gold-pressed latinum."

The Grand Nagus paused, and then he smiled. "On second thought, let's dawdle. I could use the money."

CHAPTER
15

THE TABLES WERE FULL, the conversation roaring, and the chips gleaming. Carefully wrapped decks of cards sat in front of the dealer's chairs and the dealers stood behind them waiting for Quark's signal.

Quark watched the door. Where was that Nagus? Zek would kill Quark if Quark began the game without him.

The game was already an hour late in starting and the players were getting restless. Two had come up to him to ask him if there was a problem. He had reassured them that everything was all right, that the group was only waiting for one more player. A player who had been around when Quark posted the schedule but was gone now.

The Nagus was up to something.

But then, that was what made him the Grand Nagus of all the Ferengi.

Quark wiped a hand over his brow. The environmental controls still hadn't been fixed and the room was stifling hot. The mingled smells of unwashed human bodies and strange aliens made his nostrils twitch. The stink would only grow worse as the game continued. Players would not leave their posts until their last chip was gone. By the end of the game the final two players might well have been at the table for days.

The lights went out and the conversation stopped. A group of eighty beings held their breath. Quark started counting, praying that the emergency generators would kick in. They didn't have to. By the time he reached ten, the lights were back on.

The conversation resumed, as loudly as it had been before. It almost seemed as if the players' voices were connected to the power grid.

Quark smiled at the image. Just imagine if he could shut off the conversation in the bar by pressing a button.

Someone tugged on his sleeve. He looked over to see Rom cowering beside him. Quark closed his eyes. Another problem.

Rom tugged again. Quark opened his eyes and grabbed Rom's hand. "Careful," Quark said. "You'll ruin the sweater."

"I'm sorry," Rom said. His apology came too quickly. Something *was* wrong. "I need to speak with you."

"So speak," Quark said.

"Not here," Rom said, looking around.

Quark glared at him. He didn't want to leave the room. He had a large investment to protect as well.

Finally Rom leaned over and whispered, "The signals are cutting out."

"They're doing what?" Quark shouted.

Players at the nearest two tables looked over. Quark nodded to them and grinned, feeling a panic rise in his stomach. "Ah, we were talking about the remaining player, the Nagus," he said, trying to make something up at the spur of the moment. "He, ah, is in a holosuite. We need to get him, Rom. Come along."

Quark grabbed his brother's arm and pulled him out of the room. The bar was empty, except for the Dabo girl who looked bored. Quark snapped his fingers at her. "Go stand in the door," he said. "Make sure no one leaves."

She nodded and left her station. Quark pulled Rom behind the bar itself.

"I didn't say anything about a holosuite or the Nagus," Rom said.

"I know that," Quark snapped. He kept his voice low. "What's going on with the equipment?"

Rom glanced nervously around, took a step back from Quark, and then said, "The monitors keep cutting out. The entire system just shuts down. I personally checked all the circuits again but found nothing."

A Starfleet ensign, a pretty young woman whose eyes, skin, and hair were a fine chocolate brown, peeked in the bar, apparently startled that it was empty. Quark made himself smile at her—he had been trying to catch her attention for days—but he could do no more. He couldn't even invite her in. His body was shaking with fury.

The ensign smiled back and ducked into the Promenade. Quark whirled on Rom. "The monitors were working fine two days ago. What have you done to them?"

"Nothing." Alarm made Rom's voice rise. "I have simply got them to work every time they stop."

"How long has this been going on?" Quark asked.

"Since last night," Rom said.

"And you decide to tell me now? One hour after the game should have started?"

Rom took another step back. "I thought I could fix it."

"You thought you could fix it! You thought you could fix it!" Quark grabbed Rom's earlobe and pinched so hard that Rom fell to his knees. "Fixing it means that the system works all the time. It never cuts out. It never quits. You do not repair. You improve."

Quark let go and Rom fell backwards. He clasped a hand over his red, swelling earlobe. "Right now they're working."

"Right now is not good enough," Quark said. "You must have them working all the time or I will hold you personally responsible for every hand my players lose."

"You can't do that!" Rom said. "They don't always know what's going on."

Quark froze. "They're supposed to know what's going on. Is something else wrong? Hands don't change that fast. A player can handle a flicker or two."

"That's right." Rom got up, still holding his ear. "That's right. I was wrong."

Quark grabbed his brother's elbow and pulled him closer. Rom clapped his other hand on his remaining earlobe. "You're not telling me something," Quark said.

"It's nothing important," Rom said. He was whining again. That self-pitying human sound. Quark hated it.

"It might be important to me," Quark said.

"I don't think so," Rom said.

"I do." Quark grabbed the tip of Rom's ear. Rom squealed.

"It's nothing, it's really nothing," Rom said, as he tried to wrench his ear from Quark's grasp. "It's just that the link between the players and our people watching the monitors sometimes cuts out too."

Quark let go of Rom's ear, too stunned to cause any more damage. First the Nagus, then the murder, and now this. "Are the two problems related?"

Rom massaged his ear with his thumb and forefinger. "I don't know," he said. "The systems are completely different. And one quits while the other keeps working. It makes no sense to me."

"Well, it does to me," Quark said. "Someone is sabotaging me."

"Who would do that?" Rom asked.

"I don't know." Quark kept his voice down. "But I will find out."

"You had better find out quickly," Rom said.

That brought Quark's attention back. "No! *You* had better fix the system quickly."

Rom nodded, cringing so that his shoulders protected part of his ears. The lights flickered. Both Ferengi looked up. "Maybe," Rom said, "no one is sabotaging you. Maybe that is your problem."

"Maybe," Quark said. The lights flickered again and there was a rumble as the entire station shook. "But it doesn't matter what's causing the problem. The fact is that I am going to lose a lot of money if we don't solve this right now."

Rom scuttled around the bar. "I'm sure the players will do fine on their own."

"Hah! Those two couldn't play their way out of a child's game." Quark banged his fist on the counter. "I'm stuck paying their entry fees, the Nagus, and Odo. Four hundred bars of gold-pressed latinum that I could lose if I'm not careful. And I'm not careful. I have you working on my equipment."

"Maybe you should see if you can figure out what is wrong with it," Rom said.

"And maybe you should find the Grand Nagus and order him back into the room! Idiot. I can't leave this. Go. See what you can do. Make sure the equipment works at least part of the time."

Rom hurried away from the bar as if he expected Quark to box his ears again. Quark folded his arms and leaned forward on the bar's smooth surface. Sabotage. It had to be sabotage. He had never had luck this bad before. The murder. The Nagus. Odo. And now this. All the lovely profits, disappearing as if they never had been.

Odo came around the side of the bar. Quark jumped. "I told that Dabo girl not to let anyone out of the room."

"She couldn't very well order me around, now could she?" Odo asked.

"I suppose not," Quark said.

Odo stared at Quark for a moment, as if he were trying to assess the situation. "Your players would like the game to start. They're getting quite restless."

"I'm waiting for the Nagus," Quark said.

"Ah," Odo said. "The joys of politics."

"Yeah," Quark said. "Joy. I forgot what that feels like."

"Is something wrong?" Odo asked. "You don't look like you're having any fun."

Quark slowly stood, feeling old and very tired. "Fun? Making money is fun. I wouldn't call this fun."

CHAPTER
16

THE NIGHT HAD BEEN one of the longest and most frustrating in O'Brien's career. Usually he had someone else to lean on—Geordi La Forge on the *Enterprise* for instance—someone else to take the constant questions, the constant demands, the constant pressure. What O'Brien wouldn't do to have Geordi here right now. Geordi would figure out what was causing all these problems. Geordi would have figured it out hours ago.

But of course, O'Brien was not Geordi. And Geordi had never had to deal with Cardassian technology. Sometimes O'Brien was surprised the Cardassians had ever invented the wheel, let alone their so-called advanced technology. Right now he would give anything for a top of the line Federation made warp core, instead of the Cardassian power core. Its power configuration had fluctuated all night. He was afraid

that if things continued, the core would be breached
—or it would cease functioning altogether.

O'Brien wiped his sweaty hands on the side of his
uniform. An hour ago he had had the environmental
controls working in Ops. The turbolift was functional
too. Then he had gone back to his quarters for a meal
and a much-needed shower. When he got out, dripping wet, the lights quit for nearly a minute. And the
door from the bathroom to the bedroom stuck—half-
open, fortunately. He slid through, got dressed, and
came back to Ops to find the turbolift acting up and
the replicator out. Now it felt as if the environmental
controls were down again.

None of this counted the three hours he had spent
shoring up the power core. He had just built power
levels back up to 95 percent when another wave
struck. While the station rattled, O'Brien fought to
keep the core's integrity. When the rattling ended, all
the work he had done on the core had disappeared. It
had lost 15 percent of its full power capability.

Losing power core capability wasn't bad. It was the
fluctuations. During the worst of the wave, power
levels went to 120 percent of normal. Much higher
and the core would blow. O'Brien had his best staff
near the core so that he could contact them in any
emergency. He was doing what he could from Ops.

It wasn't enough.

Maybe this was a recurring loop nightmare. Maybe
if he tried hard enough he would wake up and
everything would be fine. Maybe if he wished hard
enough he would be back on the *Enterprise* and all this
would become someone else's problem.

O'Brien slid under the engineering controls unit
and opened a panel revealing the schematics inside.

That last little bouncy rumble had knocked his entire console off-line. He found the problem—simple, really—and fixed it, then got on his feet again.

"Chief," Kira said, "I'm getting reports that all the turbolifts in the habitat ring are out."

"Let them use the stairs," O'Brien snapped.

"Not funny, Chief. At least one has passengers."

He punched the information onto his now functioning engineering center. "I'll send someone there right away." Never mind that it took staff away from other emergencies. People stuck in turbolifts sometimes made the situation worse by trying to get themselves out.

"We're getting hot up here," Sisko said as he walked behind O'Brien.

"I know that, sir."

"We shouldn't be. This Operations Center already feels like the middle of a Pletanion summer cycle."

"Yes, sir," O'Brien said. He ignored the implied command while concentrating on the turbolifts. Ops would have to wait to be comfortable.

"Another disturbance—" Dax said as the lights went out in Ops. The station rumbled as badly as it had the first time. O'Brien had to hold the console to keep from slipping. This bouncing around was not natural. Space stations did not experience turbulence.

The lights on his console remained on despite the darkness around them. How he had managed that, he would never know. He could see Dax's calm youthful face in the glow of the science console. Kira and Sisko were illuminated by the operations table. All of them took advantage of the weird lighting to see what they could discover. O'Brien abandoned the turbolift problem to monitor the power core. A power surge ran through it. A red light warned that extreme power levels could cause containment breach.

O'Brien hit his comm badge. "Teppo," he said to his best assistant, "bring power levels down in the core."

"I'm doing the best I can, sir!" Teppo's voice sounded faint over the roar of equipment. "Each bounce makes the situation worse."

O'Brien shut down all nonnecessary systems. The bouncing continued. He clung to the engineering board and ran a diagnostic outside the station. Still nothing. No visible cause.

"Teppo!" he said. "Those levels are too high."

Maybe he should have stayed near the core. Maybe he could have brought the levels down quicker. But then, he wouldn't be here to handle all the other emergencies.

"I know, sir—" The rest of Teppo's response got lost in the equipment noise.

The rumbling stopped, and the overhead lights returned. Behind him O'Brien could hear the crack and hissing of loose cables. The charred scent of fried equipment made his heart sink.

But the heat was off. Cool air was blowing through the vents.

The warning light disappeared. The power core was now operating at 75 percent of normal.

His comm badge chirruped and Teppo started speaking without waiting for O'Brien. "The surge just went away, sir," Teppo said. "We've lost twenty-five percent power."

"See what you can discover there," O'Brien said. "And before the next wave hits, let's reroute control of the core to Ops. We'll work as a unit if we have to, Ensign."

"Yes, sir."

Sisko was frowning at O'Brien. "How serious is it, Chief?"

"It's worse during those damned waves," O'Brien said. "I'd stay near the core if I knew when we were going to get hit."

"Rerouting sounds like a fine solution. That way you can work on keeping Ops operational."

O'Brien nodded. He wished he didn't have to do any of it. If only they could figure out where the turbulence was coming from.

Apparently Sisko had the same thought. "Any pattern yet?" he asked Dax.

"I'm sorry, Benjamin," Dax said.

"We're doing something wrong." Sisko pushed himself away from the operations table. His normally immaculate uniform was rumpled, and stubble covered his cheeks. He was the only member of the Ops crew who had not taken time to freshen up. "We're missing something."

"Yeah," O'Brien said, "like half the power on the station."

No one responded to his comment. He didn't expect anyone to. He put the working secondary systems back on-line.

"Maybe we're too close," Dax said.

"What does that mean?" Kira's tone was not friendly. But then, Kira's tone hadn't been friendly since the middle of the night. It seemed to O'Brien that if she could have taken a Bajoran fighting stick to all the equipment on the station she would have done so hours ago. And he would have happily helped her.

Damned Cardassians. Why couldn't they have designed something that would stand up to strange circumstances? Federation equipment did.

Most of the time.

"What I mean," Dax said, speaking in her measured way, "is that we are in the middle of this event. We know the disturbance is widespread because we know that both the Bajorans and the Cardassians have felt it. We watched the Ferengi ship disintegrate. And if this is a natural phenomenon that will pass like an ion storm, then the length of time we've been suffering under this is an indication that this thing is huge, depending, of course, on the speed it is traveling."

"What's your point, Dax?" Sisko asked.

"My point is that if we could get a runabout out of this mess and far enough away to observe, we might see the whole picture. Right now I suspect we are only getting part of the information we need."

O'Brien looked up from his engineering console. Sisko's eyes were closed, the heel of his hand pressed against his forehead. "If we send out a runabout, it runs the risk of getting destroyed like the Ferengi ship."

"Sending a runabout was not my suggestion, Benjamin," Dax said. "I don't think that's our answer at all. But we may need an outside perspective like that to understand this phenomenon. Perhaps if we contact Starfleet . . . ?"

"I've been trying," Kira said. "Our communications systems are so intermittent I don't even know which ones are functioning. I might have got through. I might not have."

A blast of ice-cold air hit O'Brien in the middle of

the back, sending shudders through him. He too had gotten no information during the disturbance. He went back to worrying about the turbolifts. Three had started working again.

"Chief," Sisko said, "we're going to need help with communications."

"For the moment," O'Brien said, without acknowledging Kira, "short-range communications are working just fine. Sending long-range subspace messages could be a problem, but I think that has more to do with the disturbance than with any problem in our systems."

"I have no evidence that communications are working," Kira said.

"Move to a different operating station," O'Brien said. "I'll fix yours as soon as I can."

Kira moved. "You're right. We have short-range. And a problem."

"Major?" Sisko said.

"A Cardassian Galor-class warship is beneath us," Dax said.

"And we're being hailed by a Bajoran ship," Kira said.

"I have it too," Dax said. "They have one of the Federation runabouts."

"Answer the Bajoran ship's hail, Major," Sisko said.

"Already done, sir," Kira said.

The turbolifts were working again. O'Brien kept an eye on the goings-on around him, in case he would have to turn his attention away from inner station problems, but he began working on the environmental controls. He was now freezing.

"Hail the Cardassian ship, Major," Sisko said. "Chief, I need to communicate with both ships at the same time. They need to talk to each other. Can you do that?"

"Can't teach pigs to fly," O'Brien muttered.

"Chief?"

"I can try, sir," O'Brien said.

"Commander," Kira said, "Bajorans and Cardassians—"

"I know how your people feel about the Cardassians, Major," Sisko said. "I don't need to be reminded of it."

O'Brien wished the communications station was working. He jury-rigged a power boost to the short-range communications systems, then opened both hailing frequencies. "I have it for you, Commander," he said, "but I won't guarantee the work for very long."

"Put them both on screen, Major," Sisko said, but by the time the words were out of his mouth, the screen had split into two distinctly different pictures. O'Brien recognized the Cardassian captain, Gul Danar. The Bajoran was Captain Litna of Planetary Defense. In her uniform and with the ship's equipment as her backdrop, she looked even fiercer than she had hours before.

"What is the meaning of this?" Litna snapped.

"Are you trying to provoke a situation, Commander?" the Cardassian asked.

"You are both in danger," Sisko said. "The last ship in this area was torn apart by the phenomenon you're both complaining about. I strongly suggest you both return home until this problem gets solved."

"Problem, Commander? If the Bajorans keep their terrorists away from our fleet—"

"You're the one attacking our planet, Gul Danar," Litna said.

"No one is attacking anyone else," Sisko said. "We are in the midst of a strange subspace phenomenon. Go home. Get your scientists busy. We need to solve this or it will destroy all of us."

"Stop protecting the Bajorans, Commander," Gul Danar shouted. "This is the last time they will terrorize us. We are here to defend ourselves. If one of our ships is attacked, we *will* begin a counterattack on Bajor."

"That is a declaration of war," Litna said.

"That is a declaration of intent," Gul Danar said. "You have already started the war."

"No one has started any war," Sisko said. "Both of you, send your ships home. We have another problem in this area of space."

"I would believe you, Commander," Gul Danar said, "if you could be more specific."

"If I could be more specific," Sisko said, "I would be. And the problem at that point might be solved. But I cannot. And I don't need the two of you squabbling like children on top of everything else."

"They have attacked our ships," Gul Danar said.

"They have ravished us for the last time," Litna responded.

"Another attack, and we will defend ourselves." Gul Danar's likeness disappeared from the screen.

"We only have a few ships, Commander," Litna said. "It would not be a contest. We rely on you for our protection. Bajor is not pleased with what has happened in the last twenty-four hours. If the situation does not change, we will not be responsible for the consequences."

Her image winked out.

"Major," Sisko said. "Bring them back."

"I don't know if talking is such a good idea right now," Kira said.

"It's the only choice we have."

The power boost surged in a ray of bright pretty colors on O'Brien's console. With a beep that wheezed out, the communications array disappeared. "Sorry," O'Brien said. "Communications are out again."

"So much for that choice," Sisko muttered. "Dax, keep searching for the cause of this turmoil. We may have a full-scale war on our hands here if we don't solve this."

Dax nodded.

Sisko turned to Kira and O'Brien. "Make getting in touch with Starfleet a priority. We are going to need help with this." He glanced around Ops. "Are the turbolifts working?"

"For the moment, sir," O'Brien said.

"Good. I'm going to take a much-needed shower. I'll be in my quarters for the next half hour should something else happen." Sisko walked to the turbolift. As he started his descent, the lights flickered.

"Chief," Dax said calmly. "My console has gone black."

O'Brien sighed. It looked as if nothing would ever be easy again.

CHAPTER
17

"ANTE, FOR HEAVEN'S SAKE." Cynthia Jones leaned back in her chair and, with her free left hand, reached behind her and caressed Dr. Bashir's neck. The good doctor jumped. Garak grimaced. The Jones woman couldn't keep her hands off the doctor although it was quite clear he wasn't interested.

Garak didn't understand why the good doctor didn't tell her to leave him alone. But then, Bashir didn't do well in social situations. Garak remembered that from the time he had asked Bashir for help. It had taken several overt instructions before the doctor understood what Garak was getting at.

Nam, the Ferengi player that Cynthia Jones had been speaking to, finally threw in his ante.

"Really," Kinsak the Romulan said. "You don't have to consider an ante, unless you want to quit the game."

Nam pressed his left ear as if it hurt him. "I wasn't

considering," he said in his sychophantic Ferengi way. "I was . . . slow."

He was up to something, and everyone at the table knew it. Kinsak and his friend Darak—who seemed remarkably calm about the murder of another Romulan—watched Nam like an Ynian Tiger watched the sweetwater gazelle it ate for dinner. Harding chomped on his Ferengi cigar, leaving yellow tobacco stains on his mouth, his gaze always assessing Nam. Klar, the other human at the table, had actually peeked at Nam's cards twice—and not very discreetly. Only the Irits appeared unperturbed, but no one could read its blank obsidian face. Garak envied it: the perfect poker face.

"Slow," Klar said. "Of course. What would one expect from a Ferengi?"

"One . . . would . . . ex-pect . . . the . . . Fer-en-gi . . . to . . . play . . . ac-cord-ing . . . to . . . its . . . own . . . rules," the Irits said. Its metallic voice grated on Garak. It sounded like the creature relied on some sort of technical device to speak the language. But try as he might, Garak couldn't see anything.

The dealer shuffled. She was a slight, human woman with dark brown hair and nimble fingers. None of the dealers were Ferengi—a shrewd move on Quark's part. No one would have trusted Ferengi dealers. Garak watched this human woman closely. He wasn't sure he could trust her either.

Still, the first two hours of play had gone well for him. He had more chips in front of him than he had when he started—a good thing, considering he had spent most of the time trying to figure out the other players' styles. That made the discomfort of the gaming room worth it. During the first hour of play, he was wondering if he would survive—not because of his hands or the other players' skill, but because the extreme heat made the temperature and the smell untenable. Even though the Meepod was three tables away, the stifling heat made her stench intensify. Garak expected everyone to become a bit ripe by the end of play, but to start out that way was a bad omen.

Then the cooling controls had kicked in. If the cold air blasts continued, the room would be an icebox by evening. At least that would control the smell.

The dealer dealt two cards to each player. Nam leaned to the left. Klar frowned at him. Cynthia Jones turned her attention from Doctor Bashir and concentrated on her hand. Garak glanced at his cards. A pair of deuces. Nice start.

Harding began the betting with five bars of gold-pressed latinum. Garak, Cynthia, the Irits, and Klar called. Both Romulans folded. Nam stared at his cards, then at the pile of chips in the center of the table.

"It's not a decision," Cynthia Jones said after a moment. "Either you call, you raise, or you fold."

Nam's hands shook as he tossed in five red chips. He leaned to the right, crowding Garak, forcing him to hold his cards close to his chest.

The dealer dealt the Flop: another deuce, a four of hearts, and a five of spades. Suddenly Nam sat up. He pressed his hand against his left ear again, and smiled. The dealer shot him a nervous glance. No one smiled in the middle of a poker hand. Nam didn't wait for Harding to start the round of betting: Nam threw in six red chips—and for the first time, his hands weren't shaking.

Garak had played with Ferengi before. They were

erratic cardplayers and often frivolous in their betting, hoping for huge profits with little effort. But Nam was very hard to read. Klar ran a hand across his silver hair, his eyes almost flat. No one else tossed in chips. Nam glanced around the table.

"Well?" he said, his tone triumphant. "You either call, raise, or fold, like the lady said."

He reached for more chips to toss in. Then, so quickly that Garak didn't see the movement, Klar grabbed Nam's wrist. "Don't be overzealous, Ferengi." Klar's voice had a flatness that matched his eyes. A chill ran down Garak's back.

For a moment, none of the players moved. Nam seemed to have shrunk into his chair. Garak frowned. Klar's comment bothered him. Perhaps because it implied a knowledge of Nam's hand and Nam's motives. Or perhaps it was the icy tone which Klar had used, that executioner's warning tone that implied that any mistake could cost the Ferengi his life.

Then the Irits grabbed six red chips and tossed them in. "Are . . . you . . . all . . . folding?" it asked.

"*I* am," Cynthia Jones said.

Harding tossed in his chips. Klar stared at Nam for a long moment, then said, "Nothing could make me fold from this round."

Garak folded despite his three deuces. The hand was not spectacular, and he felt as if he didn't want to get involved in the battle between Nam and Klar.

The dealer dealt the fourth card. Everyone stared at Nam. He watched Klar. Klar's flat expression hadn't changed. Finally, Nam folded, his hands shaking as he did so. A slight buzzing filled the air. Nam leaned over, pressing his left hand to his ear.

"Are you all right?" Garak asked.

"Earache," Nam managed. "'Scuse me." He stuck one finger in his ear. Cynthia Jones rolled her eyes.

"Disgusting," Darak said. "Remind me to never play poker with a Ferengi again."

Harding, Klar, and the Irits finished the hand while the others watched Nam. Garak barely registered the fact that Klar took the pot.

"For goodness sake, Nam, take your finger out of your ear. We're here to play poker, not watch you pick at yourself!" Cynthia Jones said. The tribble cooed, as if concurring with her words.

"Are we ready for the next hand?" the dealer asked. She shuffled the deck.

"Please," the Irits said. "Let . . . us . . . do . . . some-thing . . . be-sides . . . watch . . . this . . . ir-ri-ta-ting . . . dis-play."

"Or listen to you gag out a sentence," Klar said.

Garak frowned at the others. "I don't think it would hurt us to be polite to each other."

Kinsak shook his head. "What kind of Cardassian are you, anyway? Polite. Hah!"

The dealer finished shuffling. She set the deck in front of Cynthia Jones, who cut exactly in the middle. Then the dealer dealt the two hole cards to each player.

"I am a simple clothier," Garak said, as he picked up his cards. He had an eight of spades and a jack of hearts.

"Who stays on a Federation space station," Harding said around his cigar. He tossed in two red chips. "Hey, Klar. Are spies always polite?"

Klar put two red chips in the pot. "It's easier not to get noticed if you're polite."

"Unless you're Cardassian," Kinsak said as he checked.

"Or Klingon," Garak said with distaste. He checked as well.

So did the Irits and Cynthia Jones. Nam raised the stakes by tossing in a third red chip, and the other players did the same. They all wanted to see the Flop.

With a slight flourish, the dealer turned over the next three cards. Each card snapped as it hit the table: the three of hearts, the nine of hearts, and the ten of clubs. Garak pulled his cards closer to his chest. With the eight and the jack, he needed only one more card for a straight, but the two hearts gave another player an equally good shot at a flush. He was doing well enough. He would see how the other players bet.

Cynthia Jones folded. Nam checked, Klar raised, and the remaining players called. Nam seemed to have lost his fear as he tossed in the requisite chips. Suddenly the attention was off Garak and onto the cards themselves.

Garak was getting cold—and it wasn't just the room temperature. Nam was not acting as he had before. Sometime in the last two hands he had gained an uncharacteristic confidence. Ferengi were difficult players in the best of times, but Ferengi players in a Ferengi hosted game were always suspect. Especially if they changed their behavior.

Still, the explanation could be a simple one. Perhaps Nam's cards had improved. Or perhaps he had finally forgotten how much money sat before him, and had gotten lost in the game. Garak would bide his time and see what happened in subsequent hands.

With a smoothness that came from years of practice, the dealer turned over the next card: the queen of hearts. Garak felt a slight rush of excitement. He had his straight, but three hearts were showing. Anyone with two hearts in hand would have a flush. The straight might not be enough to beat it. When the bet came around, he pushed it by two red chips—a cautious bet, but one that signaled the other players that he would stay for the showdown.

Then Nam shoved half of his remaining chips into the pot. A small fortune in gold-pressed latinum. The chill that had been building in Garak finally overwhelmed him. Either the Ferengi played full-tilt poker, betting everything when he had a spectacular hand and whining when he didn't, or he had information he shouldn't.

But there was nothing Garak could do. He leaned back in his chair to take a moment to decide if he was going to call the bet or fold.

He didn't have to decide.

"You cheated," Klar said, his voice soft and low and very mean.

"Ferengi do not cheat," Nam said.

Garak placed his cards together, hid them in his hand, and rested his hand on the table. Then he scooted away from the two arguing players.

"Well, you do," Klar said. His gaze had that flatness again, the flatness that Garak had seen on only one other face, in the eyes of a Cardassian about to murder a prisoner.

"I have never cheated in my life!" Nam said.

"And you lie as well," Klar said.

Quark almost materialized beside the table. "Do we have a problem here?"

"You allow cheats in this game," Klar said.

"I don't cheat," Nam said, looking up at Quark.

"You know that. I am a good, honest player who simply bet too much for this hu-mon's tastes."

"He is cheating us," Klar said.

Quark looked at Klar. Garak recognized the assessing gaze. Quark had used it before to figure out how to deal with unsatisfied customers in the bar. "What proof do you have of this accusation?" Quark asked, but his tone was not belligerent—a relief, as far as Garak was concerned.

"He switched cards. You might want to search him."

Garak set his cards down. He pushed his chair back farther. He did not want to be close to this fight.

"I did not switch cards. No one would be so stupid as to do that in your tournament, Quark. I would never cheat like that," Nam said. "I—"

Quark snatched Nam's cards from his hands and studied them without letting anyone else see. Then he glanced at the cards faceup on the table. He set Nam's cards facedown, and patted Nam, making Nam turn his sleeves inside out. Quark shrugged and looked at Klar. "I see no evidence of cheating," Quark said.

Klar's expression did not change, but the room got colder.

"Did you see any cheating?" Quark asked the dealer.

She glanced at Klar before answering. Klar studied her like a Slovian water beast studied its prey. The dealer seemed unaffected. She shook her head no.

Quark bobbed at Klar, the Ferengi conciliatory gesture. "Sorry," Quark said. "But the hand must stand. If there are further problems, contact me. Finish play."

He disappeared as quickly as he had appeared. Garak pushed his chair back to the table.

Klar looked at the overlarge pot, then at Nam. Klar folded. "You will get yours, Ferengi."

Nam cackled, and tapped his bet, bouncing in his chair like an excited child. The Romulans folded, the Irits folded, and so did Garak. Nam pulled the pot toward him, his broad little face shining with greed. He had doubled his winnings with one hand.

Garak watched him. Nam had bought the pot, but it felt as if he had bought something else too. Despite the stack of chips in front of Nam, Garak did not envy him.

Not at all.

CHAPTER
18

KIRA'S HANDS WERE SHAKING. Her body was humming. She felt as if she had to keep moving or she would wilt with exhaustion. Yet at the same time, she was braced for another problem—any problem.

She focused on the communications console, making sure that O'Brien's repairs had everything on-line. She still couldn't tell if long-range communications were working. But she sent an encoded message to Starfleet, explaining the situation, and putting in a request for help.

Then she paused. Commander Sisko was gone from the bridge. O'Brien was swearing over the engineering console. Dax's fingers danced on the science console's pad, as she ran diagnostic after diagnostic. Carter pushed hair out of her face as she frowned at the operations table.

The commander had told Kira to contact Litna, but

Kira had put it off. Captain Litna had commanded a wing of Bajoran freedom fighters for years, conducting successful raids on the Cardassian strongholds. When Kira was a child, she had met Litna near the fountains and had been in awe of her ever since. Commander Sisko's handling of Litna made Kira want to crawl under the communications board. Sometimes the man didn't understand the fine points of Bajoran diplomacy.

Kira took a deep breath and hailed Litna's ship. At first no one responded. Kira bit her lower lip. Had something happened? Had the Cardassians hurt Litna? Was Litna correct? Was this all a plot?

At the second hail, Litna appeared on the main viewing screen. All activity in Ops stopped. Dax looked at Kira with a measuring gaze. Kira felt her cheeks get hot. She left the communications board and walked to Sisko's usual position in front of the operations table.

"You hailed me, Major?" Litna's tone had a trace of sarcasm, emphasis on the word *Major*.

Kira swallowed. "Yes, Captain. Commander Sisko wanted me to clarify a few things—"

"Smart man," Litna said with a smile that didn't reach her eyes. "Did he want you to speak woman to woman or Bajoran to Bajoran?"

Kira let out the breath she had been holding. "Captain, I *asked* to talk to you, since you didn't listen to him. You persist in believing that the Cardassians are attacking Bajor. They're not."

"Really, Major? Then what have we been experiencing?"

"Look," Kira said, clasping her hands behind her back. She had never encountered anyone so stubborn.

"There is some subspace activity going on that is affecting us, you, the Cardassians, and anything else in the area. A Ferengi ship broke up yesterday afternoon under the strength of this—"

"And you do not know what this phenomenon is." Litna crossed her arms in front of her chest. "Could it, in fact, be a Cardassian ploy?"

"You think they would destroy their own fleet?"

"My equipment does not show a destroyed fleet. A few ships are having problems, perhaps, but that's common." Litna leaned closer to the screen. "Tell me, Major, what is wrong with the Galor-class warship I see in Bajoran space?"

"Nothing, but—"

"You're wrong, Major." Again, Litna had a cold smile. "What is wrong is that the Cardassian warship is in Bajoran space. And the Federation—who have vowed to protect us—are doing nothing. What's worse, Major Kira Nerys, liaison between the Bajoran government and the Federation, is making apologies for both the Federation and the Cardassian ship. Unless you have forgotten, Major, you represent *Bajor.*"

Kira felt as if Litna had knocked the wind out of her. "I haven't forgotten, Captain. I just—"

"Good," Litna said. "Then solve this. For Bajor."

The screen went blank. Kira took a deep breath. Everyone in Ops was looking at her.

"For what it's worth, Major," O'Brien said, "she didn't try to understand."

Kira gripped the operations table. A few words from Captain Litna and she felt ten years old again. Kira wasn't betraying Bajor. Captain Litna wasn't listening. "Maybe I should contact her again." Kira looked down at the table. A handful of lights still indicated problems. "Try to reason with her."

"You won't be able to convince her, Major," O'Brien said. "Trust me."

"I think," Dax said, "we're better off solving whatever it is that is causing this. Then no one will believe they're under attack."

Kira nodded. They were right. All that was important at the moment was stopping the attacks, if they were attacks.

Later she would defend herself. And Litna would be very sorry she had ever doubted her.

CHAPTER
19

SCHOOL THAT MORNING had seemed too long, especially with Mrs. O'Brien talking about the children's obligations during a crisis. Children had to take care of themselves and know the safety features of the station. But they also had to remain close to home so that their parents could find them in an emergency.

Jake still hadn't followed that instruction. He had meant to return to his quarters, but Nog wanted to go back to Quark's. Jake didn't really want to hang out by the bar, but he didn't want to be alone either. Since the lights were still flickering and the environmental controls were out and the station had rocked for a third time, Jake knew his father wouldn't be in their quarters either.

Ever since they had escaped the *Saratoga* just before the Borg destroyed it, Jake had a restlessness in a crisis. He had to keep moving.

But he didn't want to be moving here, either. He and Nog stood outside the storage door with Quark's name all over it. Nog was double-checking the signals for the fifth time. Jake was afraid that Nog would push open the door and barge in.

"What are we doing?" Jake asked. "We already figured out where the signals were going."

"Don't you want to watch? I sure do," Nog said.

"Not from here," Jake said. "If anyone is inside, we'll get in real trouble."

"Yeah, I suppose," Nog said. He put the device he had been using back in his pocket. "But I really want to know what's happening. I know! Come on!"

Jake hesitated for just a moment. In his quarters he could do his homework and listen to music. Out here he and Nog could get caught or worse, they could get trapped somewhere. His father would never find him.

"Come on!" Nog said.

Jake followed, tucking his homework padd under his arm. He would go along for a few minutes and then he would leave. Maybe he would be able to convince Nog to teach him how to play poker—in Jake's quarters.

They stopped at the edge of the Promenade. Nog took out the device and frowned. "Look!" he said.

Jake looked. Instead of glowing red, the screen was bleeping. "What does that mean?"

"There are two sets of signals. One of them goes to the storage room, but one of them goes farther down the corridor. It's strange."

That caught Jake's attention. "Two sets of signals?"

Nog nodded.

"Is that storage room just a decoy?"

"I don't know," Nog said. "But I'm going to find out."

"Jake!"

Jake closed his eyes. His father. He had never expected his father here. Jake turned and opened his eyes. "Hi, Dad."

"I thought I told you to be in our quarters when things were wrong at the station."

"I was going there," Jake said, his voice trailing off. He hadn't been there yet, and the schoolroom was closer to their quarters than he was right now.

Nog stood beside him, arms pressed against his side. The device had disappeared, probably into a pocket. Jake's father looked exhausted. He hadn't shaved and his uniform was rumpled. Jake hadn't seen his dad look like that in a long time.

"You're a long way from our quarters," his dad said.

"I know." Jake looked at his feet. Then his gaze caught his homework padd. "But we had school this morning, and Nog and I were going to get a little something to eat in the Replimat."

Jake's dad glanced around. "Well, all right. Maybe for a few minutes. But do go back. I would like to know where you are."

Jake bit his lower lip. "Are you going home to stay for a while?"

"Afraid not. I have some things to check on in Quark's. Then I'm going home to shower and shave," his father said. "Then I have to get back to Ops."

"Oh," Jake said. If his father had been going directly to their quarters, Jake would have gone along.

Then he would have told him about the cheating. In fact, he could now. "Dad?"

"Yes, son?"

"You know about the game in Quark's?"

Sisko sighed and nodded. "That's one of the reasons I'm going there."

Nog grabbed Jake's arm, just tight enough to warn him. Jake couldn't say anything in front of his friend. "Can I come with you?"

"I'm afraid Quark's is not a place I want you to go," his father said. "Especially right now."

"Okay," Jake said. He couldn't keep the disappointment from his voice. Maybe he would go to the Replimat and then home. He did have a lot to do. "I'll see you later, then."

His dad squeezed his shoulder.

"Jake!" Nog said. "I forgot my padd upstairs."

Jake glanced at Nog. He hadn't carried a homework padd since the Nagus's last visit. Jake sighed. "Okay," he said. "Let's get it and then go to the Replimat."

Nog started up the stairs into the Promenade. Jake followed. He stopped halfway up the steps and looked down. His father was walking slowly past the shops, surveying the entire area. Always the commander, always seeing what was going on. Maybe Jake should have told him about the strange signals. But maybe his father already knew.

"Come on!" Nog said. He was already up the stairs by the access portal. Jake sighed. He went up the remaining stairs and hurried over. Nog was opening the portal.

"You coming?" he asked.

Jake peered over the stairs. His father was looking

inside Odo's closed office and frowning. "I guess so," Jake said.

"Well, better do it now. You wouldn't want your father to catch us." He crawled inside. Jake followed and reached for the portal. It would only be for a few minutes. And then he would go home.

No matter what.

CHAPTER
20

"IT *AMAZES ME*," said Berlinghoff Rasmussen, his voice blaring over the murmured conversation, "the way some things disappear over the centuries and others remain."

Bashir sighed and stacked his chips. Rasmussen, a lanky, balding man with a commanding voice, seemed to believe he had the duty to entertain the entire table. Bashir would have preferred quiet conversation with Sarlak, the Vulcan who sat beside him.

"I mean, take poker. A human game that has spread all over the galaxy. My ancestors played it, for god's sake, and since I'm at least two centuries older than anyone else here—"

"You should play a much wiser game than the rest of us," the Bajoran named Pera snapped. He sat beside Rasmussen and seemed as put out by Rasmussen's constant conversation as Bashir was.

Rasmussen wasn't a bad sort. He was, from what Bashir could gather, a bit of a con artist who had arrived on the *Enterprise* in a time machine a few years ago, claiming to be from the future, when he was in fact from the past.

He never said, but Bashir deduced that the time machine had been stolen. Rasmussen had obliquely referred to the fine treatment on twenty-fourth-century rehab colonies. He had to have stayed in a few to know that.

"Games of chance exist in most developed cultures," Sarlak said. He templed his fingers and watched as the dealer shuffled.

"Even on Vulcan?" asked Haurk, the Ferengi who sat on Bashir's left. His tone implied that such a thing was unheard of.

"Vulcan abandoned such pleasures many centuries ago," said a Romulan from the next table.

Sarlak ignored the comment. "Our culture enjoys studying many things about the universe," he said. "Game theory is one of them. Which is why I'm here. I specialize in games of constantly shifting odds, such as poker."

"What *I* have been wondering is how you manage to bluff," Rasmussen said. "I thought Vulcans never bluffed."

"Really," Bashir said. "That is a tasteless question. You're asking Sarlak to explain his betting strategy."

Sarlak put his hand on Bashir's arm. "No, he is asking an important theoretical problem that has bothered Vulcan games theorists for a long time. While it is true that Vulcans do not bluff, neither does anyone else in poker."

"Knock it off, Pops," Pera said. "Everyone bluffs in poker."

Sarlak nodded. "That is the poker parlance, yes. If you consider bluffing to be a claim that you will perform an action you do not intend to, then you are correct, Vulcans do not bluff. But, in poker, bluffing has a different meaning. Players play to win. Poker players use the bluff as a strategy for winning. In poker, you win by claiming that you can win and having other players believe you. Or not believe you. Since the action is understood by all to be a potential ruse, it is not really a ruse at all."

Bashir grinned and leaned back. "I think I got that," he said.

"Well, I didn't," Rasmussen said. "Sounds like a lot of rationalization to me."

"Actually," Sarlak said, "many fine Vulcan minds have spent centuries pondering this issue. I am here to test it."

And he had been testing it well. He clearly was not a traditional poker player, Bashir thought, but his comments made sense. Sarlak played a very odds-friendly game with little bluffing, and had managed, so far, to do quite well for himself.

Better than the Romulan who had joined them at the table and frowned when he saw a Vulcan present. The Romulan had informed them all that he was the best player at the table. None of them complained when the Romulan was the first to lose all his chips. When he lost the final pot to Sarlak, the Romulan had thrown his hole cards at the dealer and stalked out of the room. The tension at the table had lessened considerably after that.

Bashir missed the company of the second casualty

of the table. An old freighter captain, who had traded stories with Rasmussen, had played well, but had had marginal cards. When he lost his final chip he stood, bowed, and wished everyone better luck than he had. So far his wish had almost come true.

Bashir's holdings had only decreased by about two thirds. Yet he knew he had enough to stay in any big hand and get back to being ahead. Sarlak was holding even, but Bashir figured his play was too predictable. He would probably lose a little each hand from now on and be out of the game by morning. Pera seemed to be doing all right in chips, but Bashir figured he would be the next to go. He played aggressively, but unwisely at times, holding onto cards when he should have folded.

The two Ferengi worried Bashir the most. They were terrible players, often betting a small fortune on a pair of deuces, but they had had a string of luck that seemed uncanny. Haurk's luck in the last hand had returned him to his original stake.

"Each century seems to have developed stories about its most famous poker players," Rasmussen said, obviously trying to change the subject, and return the focus of the conversation to himself.

"Most of us don't care about stories." Pera ran a hand through his dark hair. "Just the game."

"I think someone should cut," Bashir said, as the dealer set the cards on the table. He didn't want to hear the stories any more than Pera did.

"Some of those stories are fascinating," said Sarlak, "and led to ways that the game evolved."

Morn, the rather silent, lumpy alien who often traded jokes with Quark in the bar, reached across

Rasmussen and cut. The movement was illegal, but no one protested. They all wanted the game to continue.

"My father used to tell of an uncle who—"

"Pardon me," Bashir said, "but let's leave the story-telling for a moment while we play out the hand."

The dealer dealt the hole cards. Bashir waited until the second card was dealt before picking them up. He had a mild superstition about waiting until all his cards were in front of him before examining them. The habit began in childhood, when he believed that touching the cards before it was time ruined his luck. Sometimes, late in a game, that old belief returned.

The dealer set her deck down and waited. Bashir was the last to scoop up his cards. The ace and king of spades. What wonderful luck! This would be the hand that would catch him up. He just felt it.

He was reaching for his chips when the entire room went black. Pitch-black. He couldn't even see the cards in front of his face.

The room fell into a shocked silence.

"Cards down!" Quark's voice boomed. No backup lights were coming on. Wasn't this room equipped with emergency preparations? "Hands on your own chips. And please remain that way until the lights come back up."

Bashir set his cards down and gathered his chips against him. He knew that Sarlak wouldn't touch the chips, but he didn't trust the Ferengi. Or Pera for that matter.

"Rom!" Quark's voice held that bossy, obnoxious tone he used with his brother. "Where are those emergency lights?"

Rom's response was lost in the growing conversation. Once everyone in the room realized that the lights weren't coming back on right away, mutters of dissatisfaction began.

"—stupidity of playing in a place designed by Cardassians—"

"—what if we're under attack?—"

"—some ploy by the Ferengi to steal all our money—"

"—Krax! Where is my idiot son? Krax!—"

Above the snatches of conversation, Bashir caught a steady, menacing cursing. The hair rose on the back of his neck. The lights had been out the night before, when Naralak died.

A chair fell over behind him. He turned in the direction of the noise just as the lights came back on.

Bashir blinked in the brightness.

A Ferengi was on the floor beside his table, twisting in pain. Bashir could see the blood from where he sat.

Odo had left his chair near the door and was hurrying across the room. Quark was behind him.

Bashir jumped up. "Watch my chips," he said to Sarlak. Sarlak nodded.

Garak, the clothier, was sitting in a chair near the Ferengi, his hands raised as if to protect himself. He half-stood when Odo got there, then hovered. Bashir pushed him aside and kneeled beside the bleeding Ferengi who tried to sit up.

"No," Bashir said, gently pushing him back. "Stay down." He quickly checked the wounds. The entry was clean—not ripped. Stab wounds from a knife with a smooth edge, like those that had killed Naralak the day before.

But Nam had been somewhat lucky. The attacker

had had no knowledge of Ferengi physiology. The four wounds would have been instantly fatal to a human— and would have put a Romulan in critical condition. A Klingon might not have survived either, but Ferengi physiology was very different from other species. Bashir worked quickly to slow the bleeding of the wounds beneath the rib cage and across the stomach. It appeared the Ferengi's heart might have been grazed. He was going to need help quickly.

"Ops!" Odo almost shouted into the intercom. "Transport two at once to the infirmary."

"No!" Bashir shouted. "He's too weak to transport." Bashir slapped his comm badge. "Medical assistance to Quark's. Stat!"

"Anyone see anything?" Odo said to those standing and sitting nearby, staring intently at each one.

Bashir glanced around at the shaking heads. Then he focused on stopping Nam's bleeding.

"Klar was claiming the Ferengi had cheated him," Garak said.

"Klar?" Odo asked.

"He *was* cheating me," Klar said.

Bashir put pressure on the wounds, staunching the blood flow. His hands were big enough to cover two wounds at once. Fortunately Nam was small, even for a Ferengi. Then Bashir looked up.

Odo stepped toward Klar and Klar retreated.

"So you tried to kill him?" Odo asked.

Klar shook his head. "Why would you think I did it?"

"For a start," Odo said, "from the bloodstains on your hands."

Bashir was shocked at the speed the knife appeared

in Klar's hand. It had the blood of the Ferengi still fresh on its blade.

Odo reached for the knife, but Klar was quick. He thrust hard at Odo's stomach.

Odo didn't even flinch or try to jump back. His stomach turned into fluid metal and the knife and hand passed right through.

Then, as the shocked Klar tried to withdraw his weapon, Odo grabbed him above the elbow and with a quick twist sent the knife bouncing across the floor in front of Bashir. Nam flinched, but Bashir gripped him tightly and peered at the weapon. It was the same type of knife that had killed Naralak.

Klar struggled in Odo's grasp, but couldn't free himself.

Odo yanked hard on the man's arms to stop the struggle. "I believe that Starfleet will have your records under the name . . . L'sthwan. Am I right?"

Nam gasped and then choked and Bashir turned his full attention back to his patient. He should have brought his medical kit to the game. He had thought about it, but ruled it out. What was taking his medical team so long?

"Nam?" Quark crouched beside Bashir.

"You're in my light," Bashir snapped. Then, seeing the concern on Quark's face, he softened. "I'm doing everything I can. He'll be all right once I get him to the infirmary."

Quark nodded thanks to Bashir and then looked up at Klar, or L'sthwan, if that was his name. "You tried to kill Nam for cheating you?"

"I understand that cheating is the way of your race," L'sthwan said. "Perhaps genocide is in order."

His voice was flat and cold and sent shivers down

Bashir's spine. If he had a chance he would run a psychological battery on the man. But he knew what he would find.

"Quark settled a dispute between the two of them over cheating an hour ago," Garak said.

Odo snorted. "It doesn't look as if he did it very well." He shoved L'sthwan toward the door. "But I have settled it for good."

CHAPTER
21

SISKO HESITATED A MOMENT before stepping into the Promenade. He glanced behind him at the stairs where his son had disappeared. Jake had seemed odd, a little more reserved than normal, and younger than usual. He hadn't asked to be with Sisko during a crisis in a long time.

The stairs were empty. He couldn't see his son. Sisko sighed. Times like these they both needed Jennifer. She would have taken care of Jake while Sisko took care of the station.

But she was gone. He still had trouble with that, even with the acceptance he had reached shortly after he arrived on Deep Space Nine. He was raising their son alone.

He hoped Jennifer approved of the job he was doing.

He wasn't sure he approved sometimes.

He walked into the Promenade. All of the stores were closed. Garak had changed his clothing display and his CLOSED sign blocked much of the door. How unusual. When Garak didn't want business his store was usually dark. Most of the other stores had signs that read CLOSED DUE TO STATION REGULATIONS.

Some of the stores had printed those signs when it became clear that the Federation insisted on certain behavioral principles from shopkeepers. Many of them had had to close their operations for short periods of time just to meet those regulations. The shopkeepers had kept the signs and often used them whenever a station crisis occurred.

Only Quark's remained open. Open and empty. The game had to be going on in a back room.

Sisko was alone on the Promenade. The handful of people he had seen as he was approaching had disappeared. He heard a very faint buzz of conversation, but it appeared to be coming from Quark's.

He was about to step inside when the lights went off. A faint beeping let him know that a turbolift was stuck. The smell of rotted flesh, mixed with roses, reached him. How odd. What would cause an odor like that?

He grabbed onto the wall near the entrance, more to keep his bearings than for support. This darkness was absolute. He didn't know why the Cardassians had never installed emergency lighting in the Promenade. He had asked O'Brien to do so in his spare time, but with the problems in the station, O'Brien never had spare time. Sisko would have to make the lighting a priority soon.

"Come on, O'Brien," he whispered. "Let's get some light here."

The noise behind him had grown louder. Apparently the people he couldn't see in Quark's didn't like the darkness either. He didn't want to move while it was still dark, but he would if it lasted too much longer.

Then the lights came back up. Sisko let out his breath. Normally darkness didn't bother him, but with all the unexplained problems, he worried each time the lights went out. All he needed was the entire station to malfunction permanently. He hoped Kira would be able to reach Starfleet sometime soon. He needed help here.

He glanced around. The fact that the Promenade was empty—despite all that'd been happening—bothered him. Voices rose in Quark's. Sisko stepped inside.

The Dabo girl was standing beside the table, peering at a closed door near the back. The voices were coming from there.

"Is the game still going on back there?" Sisko asked.

The Dabo girl started. She smoothed her scanty metallic dress against her skin. "Commander," she said, her voice shaking.

Sisko couldn't remember if he had ever spoken with her before. She had always been supervising a game when he had come to Quark's, laughing and shouting "Dabo!" with the players.

"Well?" he asked.

She opened her mouth and then closed it.

"It's a poker game, sir."

"I know that," Sisko said.

"It's closed, sir."

"I don't want to play. I would just like to speak to Quark."

"Oh." She laughed, and he recognized that full-throated sound. He had heard that often enough. "Sorry. I'll get him."

"Wait," Sisko said. Actually Quark wouldn't do him any good. "Where's Odo?"

"In there." The Dabo girl pointed at the closed door.

"Tell him I want to see him."

"Yes, sir!" she said. She moved away from the Dabo table as the door hissed open. The low conversation he had heard since he arrived in the Promenade got louder and that rotted roses smell grew stronger. The smell was mixed with human body odor, Ferengi sweat, and Deluvian coffee.

Sisko turned. Through the door he saw about fifty people, most sitting at tables. Quark was standing, wringing his hands. A greenish Meepod sat near the back, the source of the rotted flesh smell. Odo was making his way through the door, his hand firmly holding the arm of a tall, broad-shouldered human male.

Three members of Doctor Bashir's staff bumped Sisko as they hurried by him, each carrying a medical kit. They ran toward the back of the room where Bashir stood.

"What's happening, Constable?" Sisko asked when Odo got close to him.

"We have found the infamous L'sthwan," Odo said. "Almost at the expense of one of Quark's Ferengi friends."

L'sthwan struggled in Odo's grasp. "He had no right to take me from the game, Commander."

"Actually," Sisko said, "he has every right. Is the Ferengi seriously injured?"

Odo nodded. "Bashir assures us that he will live."

"Unfortunately," L'sthwan said, "the little bastard cheats."

"He's a Ferengi," Sisko said. "They're more interested in profit than rules."

L'sthwan smiled. "And what are you interested in, Commander?"

"Getting you off my station," Sisko said.

"And yet you can't. You seem to be having problems."

"You're very astute," Sisko said. He didn't like the man. Odo needed to get him to the brig. Sisko turned to go.

"In your readings," L'sthwan said, "have you discovered a subspace fluctuation accompanied by solitrium waves?"

Sisko stopped and peered at L'sthwan. Dax had been getting solitrium waves, among many others, during each incident. "Yes, we have," Sisko said.

"Well, well," L'sthwan said. "The Ghost Riders are ranging pretty far from home."

"Ghost Riders?" Sisko asked.

L'sthwan smiled and rocked back on his heels. Sisko had seen that look before. L'sthwan wanted something.

"Are you saying you know what's causing these problems in the station?" Odo asked.

"I believe you need my help, Commander," L'sthwan said, ignoring Odo. "But I have a price for the information I give you."

"And that is?" Sisko asked.

"Let me finish the game and keep my winnings."

"He can't play!" Odo said. "He kills anyone whom he suspects of cheating."

Sisko looked at Odo. Odo had been locked in Quark's. He didn't realize how vital this information was. "Well, then, Constable, that is something you will have to deal with."

"You'll let me continue playing?" L'sthwan asked.

"Only if you give me information I need," Sisko said.

"We have a deal?" L'sthwan asked.

"You may keep your earnings if you win," Sisko said. "You will need them when you stand trial for the murder you committed here."

"Fine," L'sthwan said.

"So—" Sisko moved over to a table and motioned to Odo to let L'sthwan sit down. L'sthwan sat and so did Sisko. "Tell me about the Ghost Riders."

"Well," L'sthwan said, leaning back in the chair as if he and Sisko were old friends. "I first encountered them on the far side of this sector. I was in a supply ship heading back from a tournament on Risa. The ship was nearly destroyed in a fashion that reminds me of this. The old trader who piloted the thing managed to get us out of the area. Then he told me about the Ghost Riders."

Odo paced behind the chair. He kept sending Sisko pointed glances. Odo clearly did not like having L'sthwan out in the open.

"Go on," Sisko said.

"The old guy said that the Riders couldn't see us. They use special ships that function slightly out of phase, and their prototype phase shifters cause violent subspace distortions. They're hunting an energy crea- ture that they call *Espiritu*. Capturing one of the beings alive brings the Riders a huge profit." L'sthwan grinned. "I've been studying the Riders. I would love to go on one of their hunts with them."

"They would let you?" Sisko asked.

"They let anyone, for a large enough fee. Even you, Commander."

"This information does not help you, Commander," Odo said. "Let me take him to the brig. He doesn't need to play anymore."

"It was an interesting story," Sisko said. "But you haven't told me how to save my station."

"It's quite simple," L'sthwan said. "You move it, or hold on until they're gone."

"I would prefer to communicate with them," Sisko said.

L'sthwan laughed. "Can you make this station vibrate to the exact wavelength as those solitrium waves? I would doubt it. It would take more energy than even the *Espiritu* have. No, Commander. You have to send someone to Risa. The Riders have a small headquarters there, where they take funds for the next hunt. Ask them to stay out of this area. But, of course, that won't do much good. They go where the *Espiritu* go."

"And they can't see us because they're out of phase?"

"That's right," L'sthwan said. He stood. "The game will start up again soon. I would like to go back."

"I'm sure you would," Sisko said. "Is that all you know about these Ghost Riders?"

"I can tell you where to find them on Risa."

Odo stopped pacing. He put his hand back on L'sthwan's arm.

"That doesn't do me much good," Sisko said, "since I'm here."

L'sthwan shrugged. "But the rest of the information will help you, Commander. Now, if you could get your flunky to take me back to the card room—"

Odo grew two inches, obviously angry.

"I don't think so," Sisko said. "Odo, be nice to our friend L'sthwan in the brig. Give him anything he wants. Cards, food, whatever he needs. And if he thinks of more about the Ghost Riders, contact me."

Odo nodded. His expression didn't change, but Sisko could see the pleasure tugging at the corners of Odo's features. He tapped his comm badge. "Primmon. Meet me in the brig. I have the guest you were looking for."

"We had a deal!" L'sthwan shouted, as Odo began dragging him away.

Sisko shook his head. "I don't make deals with murderers," he said flatly.

"You said I could keep playing."

Sisko smiled widely and leaned closer to L'sthwan as if telling him a secret of great importance. "I was bluffing."

CHAPTER
22

THE SERVICE AREA was hot and smelled of dust. Jake stifled a sneeze as he crawled in. Light filtered up from the rooms below, but the holosuites were wonderfully quiet. Jake's big fear as he passed them had always been that he would hear something he didn't want to hear.

Nog was ahead of him, walking almost upright now that they had gone past the holosuites. Nog had brought a tiny Ferengi single beam flashlight and was using it to illuminate their way.

"No sense in stepping on equipment," he had told Jake with a grin.

Jake's heart was pounding. He should have said something to his father. He would as soon as they got out of this. Maybe he should have followed his father to their quarters and talked to him there.

Nog had just turned on the service walkway in the

opposite direction of the back room. He held the light in one hand and his father's device in the other. Nog thought he knew where the secret room was, but he wasn't taking any chances. Jake thought the whole trip was too much of a chance.

"Almost there," Nog hissed.

Good. This was the second pair of pants Jake had stained with dust and dirt from these service ways. He didn't like being up here, with the faint hum of running equipment, the thin planking that served as a floor, and the odd lights coming through from the rooms below.

Nog's flashlight barely cut through the darkness in front of them. Jake wanted to see more than four feet away. What if Chief O'Brien hadn't finished working on this part of the station yet? What if this walkway just ended?

Then, from below, all the lights went out. Jake froze. He thought it had been dark before. Now the only thing he could see was Nog, illuminated in the thin beam of the Ferengi flashlight.

"Wow," Nog said. "Power's down again."

He kept moving forward. Jake didn't move for a moment, but the light got fainter and fainter. He didn't want to be caught in the complete dark.

He followed, slowly. "Be careful," he said more to himself than to Nog. If either one of them stepped off the walkway they would fall through the ceilings of the rooms below. At best, it would be embarrassing; at worst, they could get hurt.

"I know what I'm doing, hu-mon," Nog said, turning to grin at Jake. Nog's slight movement was enough to throw him off balance. He swung his arms, making the light circle the area like a strobe, illuminating walls, ceiling, walkway, floor.

Jake reached for him and caught Nog's arm. Nog took a step backwards to regain his balance. Something crunched, then Nog toppled even farther. His foot had gone through the floor. Or, more accurately, the ceiling of the room below.

"What is that?" a panicked voice said from below.

"Something fell on me!" someone else said.

Nog leaned backwards and pulled Jake toward him. Jake braced himself on the walkway, feeling like they both hung over the edge of a cliff. Nog's left arm was flung behind his head, the light illuminating a plastic coated far wall. With his right hand, he grabbed Jake's shirt.

Then Nog's other leg slipped through the floor. Jake held on with all of his strength.

"The ceiling is caving in!" someone yelled.

"Let's get out of here!"

"It might be just as bad outside."

"We can't leave the equipment!"

"Hold on!" Jake hissed.

"I am holding on," Nog said.

The lights came back on. The darkness no longer seemed dark. Nog's chest glowed with the lights from below. His legs hung through the floor, and his hips were trapped in the flooring. Now that Jake could see the problem, he knew how to solve it. He braced himself and tugged. Nog popped out of the hole like a hot dog squeezed out of a bun. He scrambled onto the walkway, and both boys peered into the room below.

Eight Ferengi faces looked up at them. Most of the Ferengi had pieces of ceiling and dust coating their bald heads. All the Ferengi were frowning.

"Let's get out of here," Nog whispered.

Jake didn't have to be told twice. He pushed himself to his feet and ran along the service walkway. His footsteps clanged, and Nog's clanged too in an off-rhythm. Jake's breath caught in his throat. The Ferengi were yelling behind them and arguing about how to get into the ceiling.

When he reached the narrow part of the passage, Jake flung himself onto his knees, wincing as a jolting pain ran through his body. Those scrapes would be terrible. He crawled as fast as he could to the access panel. Nog was right behind him, breathing hard.

The panel loomed ahead. Jake pushed it with all his strength, and then dove out of it. Nog followed, tucking and rolling across the floor like a ball.

Jake slammed the portal shut and ran, imagining that at any moment he would hear the pounding of an army behind him.

CHAPTER
23

KIRA HAD PUNCHED IN half a message to Starfleet before a squeal from the communications board let her know that long-range subspace still wasn't working. O'Brien had managed to get the board up and running, so Kira felt better working at her old station. But still she found nothing more frustrating than running to fix equipment that was constantly breaking down.

With no end in sight.

She had barely eaten since the crisis started. She was surviving on water and an occasional sweet. She had gone beyond tired—she was focused, as she had been in those early days of fighting the Cardassians on Bajor. She would run on pure adrenaline until someone would stop her and force her to sleep.

She had hated sleeping. Sleeping meant she would miss something. In those days, if she missed something, thing, she might lose her life.

This crisis felt the same way. They had been lucky. So far the power core had held and life support had only gone down for short periods of time. Having the environmental controls constantly fail was hard enough on them. Right now Ops was so cold that she shivered every time she moved.

She did like being cold better than being warm. Being warm made her tired, and she didn't need to be tired.

"Reports in," O'Brien said. "Engineering has fixed docking rings four and five. The ships docked there will be stable now."

"Also," Carter said, "the airlock on docking ring sixteen will now open."

"I'm sure the Ferengi who was stuck in there is glad to be out," Kira said. She fiddled with the communications board. Nothing had worked so far to reestablish long-range communications. She was actually repeating her actions. She wondered if anyone else was doing the same.

The hum of the turbolift took her focus off the board. Sisko was back. He still hadn't been to his quarters. His uniform was as rumpled as it was when he left, and from this distance his five o'clock shadow made his face look bruised. Oddly, though, he seemed to have more energy than he had when he left.

"Didn't expect you back so soon," Kira said.

"Sir," O'Brien said with a bit of a grin. "You were supposed to shower."

"I will," Sisko said. He strode across Ops to the science console. "Has anyone heard of the Ghost Riders?"

"Solitrium waves!" O'Brien said, as if that connection made sense. "How could I have missed it?"

"You mean you know what's going on?" Kira leaned forward on her console.

"Maybe," O'Brien said. "Dax, let me at the science console."

"Certainly." Dax stood. "What are Ghost Riders, Benjamin?"

"Have you heard of them, Chief?" Sisko asked.

"Just a reference back when I was on the *Enterprise.*" His fingers flew over the board. "Let me see if I can access any information about them."

"While he's looking," Kira said, her frustration making her bounce on the balls of her feet, "tell us what you know."

"I don't know much," Sisko said. "Odo arrested a man down at Quark's who claimed that Ghost Riders were causing the station's problems. The man was bargaining to stay out of the brig, and the story was strange enough that I thought perhaps he was making it up."

"I don't think so, Commander," O'Brien said. "Just give me a minute."

They didn't have a minute. Not now, when they were close. The exhaustion that Kira had been holding at bay threatened behind her eyes. "What are these things?" she snapped, angry that she had had to ask twice.

"My source says they are hunting what he called 'energy creatures.'"

"Energy creatures?" Dax asked.

"Espiritu?" Kira leaned against the console. "They're hunting *Espiritu?"*

Sisko turned. "You know of them, Major?"

"Of course," Kira said. "Every Bajoran child has heard of them. They were discovered near here when I was about five." She ran her fingers through her short hair. "They're gentle, harmless creatures. I can't believe that someone would hunt them."

"I have had no evidence of life-forms on my sensors," Dax said, her hands flying across the science pad.

"You wouldn't," Kira said. "They live out of phase from us. They can pass through most things, unseen and unfelt."

She sighed. She had learned as much about them as she could. As a child, she had wanted to pass through things unseen and unfelt. When she had joined the resistance against the Cardassians, she had longed to find a way to be like the creatures, so that all of Bajor would disappear from the Cardassians' grasp.

"I found it," O'Brien said. "Ghost Riders use a loose group of runabout-sized, single-manned ships. They roam space together like a pack of wild animals. There is no record of them ever working in this area before, but they are wanted by the Federation on a long list of charges. They were tagged with the name Ghost Riders because their ships function just out of phase with normal space. The Romulans were using the same technology in an attempt to perfect an improved cloaking device. The Ghost Riders stole the technology from them."

The last brought Kira back from the past. "Why would they?" she asked. "I heard about that new cloaking device. It doesn't work."

"It must work," Sisko said. "The Ghost Riders are using it."

"It doesn't work for the Romulans, sir," O'Brien said. "There are too many problems. The worst one is that when a ship is out of phase—which is how it is cloaked—it can't figure where it is in real space."

"So it's flying blind," Sisko said. "Are the Ghost Riders flying blind?"

"Not really," O'Brien answered. Kira had the picture now. The Ghost Riders had found a way to be in the same phase as the *Espiritu*. They actually got to see the beautiful pulsing glow that Kira had just heard about. And they were hunting it. She clenched her fists. Just like the Cardassians. They found something beautiful, so they wanted to destroy it. "The Ghost Riders aren't concerned about our space. They want to follow the *Espiritu*. In that phase, they can see them just fine."

"How do the solitrium waves figure in?" Dax asked.

O'Brien moved away from her board and went back to his, speaking as he went. "Holding the ships out of phase creates strange effects in the normal space around them. That was another problem of the Romulan cloaking device. The ships weren't really cloaked because they could be tracked by the changes in space around them. One of those changes was solitrium waves."

Dax took her place at the science console, but did nothing except watch O'Brien. "So," she said, "the side effects from the Ghost Riders are creating our problems."

"It would seem that way," Sisko said.

"I'm not sure, sir," O'Brien said. "We don't know what they're doing to those energy creatures."

"I'm sure they're killing them," Kira said. Destroying all the freedom. Just because they were beautiful. She hated that kind of injustice.

"Perhaps," Dax said. "But for what?"

"My source mentioned that when caught alive, the *Espiritu* were worth a lot of money."

"Alive?" O'Brien said. "Could they be bleeding off the energy, then?"

Dax had again focused on her console. "Solitrium waves are increasing," she said. "Would that mean—?"

The station rocked. As the lights flickered, Kira moved to an engineering station. Warning lights flooded the board. The environmental controls shut off. The cold air against her back was gone. Sisko staggered, then caught himself on the edge of the science console.

"Life support out in docking ring five," Kira said.

"All the doors in the living quarters on level six jammed," Dax said.

"Replicators out in the Promenade," Carter said.

"The power core has reached 150 percent of normal," O'Brien said.

"The system can't sustain that!" Sisko whirled. He hit his comm badge. "Mr. Teppo, take that core off-line."

Kira turned her attention to the power core. Around its icon on the pad, a red warning light flashed.

"Core breach in one minute," the computer said.

"I'm trying here, sir," O'Brien said. "I can't get to the core."

"Commander," Teppo's voice sounded tinny through the comm link, "we're losing containment."

The trembling stopped.

"Solitrium waves receding," Dax said.

The red light around the power core winked off.

"Power core fluctuating," O'Brien said. After a short pause he continued, "It's now fifty percent of normal and holding."

"How's that containment, Mr. Teppo?" Sisko asked.

"I see no serious damage," Teppo said, "but I'll run a quick diagnostic."

Kira brushed her hair off her forehead. "Commander, Cardassian technology is very fussy. If we don't figure out what to do about the power core, it could blow."

"It won't blow until it holds 75 percent over normal for thirty seconds," O'Brien snapped.

"Which," Sisko said, "it just might do the next time we get hit. Chief, I want you to double-check the containment fields and see what you can do about shutting the core down at a moment's notice."

O'Brien nodded. Kira put her hands on the small of her back and stretched. They had better find a solution quickly. She had seen the devastation from a blown Cardassian power core once, many years before. It had taken out twenty square kilometers of ground along with the military research station which housed the core. It was not a pretty sight.

She took a deep breath and turned her attention to her console. She brought the life-support systems back up in the docking ring, then turned her attention to the doors. The problem looked big enough that the solution might not be possible from Ops.

"Benjamin," Dax said, her voice tinged with a slight amount of panic. "The Cardassian ship is breaking up."

Kira moved back to communications. "The Cardassians are shouting about being attacked. Litna is ignoring them. I can't hail either one of them."

"Is the tractor beam working?" Sisko asked O'Brien.

"No, sir." O'Brien frowned as he punched the pad. "I'll see what I can do."

"We need to help the Cardassians, Benjamin," Dax said. "It's a mess out there."

Kira's fingers slowed on the console. She had an obligation to save lives, but it was harder to work for Cardassian lives.

"How many on board?" Sisko asked Kira.

"Too many to beam over, even if all the transporters were working correctly."

"Chief, get a lock on as many people as you can."

"I'm trying, sir, but the interference is getting in our way."

"We're running out of time, Benjamin," Dax said. "Their ship is falling apart."

"Two shuttles have just left the Cardassian ship," Kira said. "They have about five more on a ship of that size."

"Let's hope they make it," Sisko said. "Since we can't seem to help them."

"The five other shuttles are out too," O'Brien said.

"That's it for the ship," Dax said. "It's breaking up."

A light blinked on the communications console. "A message coming in from Captain Litna," Kira said. "She complains of Cardassian attack, then thanks us for destroying the Cardassian ship. She says she is returning to Bajor for repairs but she will return."

"On screen." Sisko walked down the steps to the front of the operations table.

Kira shook her head. "She has blocked any response, sir. She does not want to communicate, just to let us know what she thinks. We are being hailed by one of the Cardassian shuttles too, sir."

"Can we put that on screen, Major?"

Kira didn't appreciate the sarcasm. She opened the channel and put the Cardassian vessel on screen. On the eye-shaped screen, Gul Danar appeared. Dirt covered his ugly Cardassian face.

"Such an attack violates our treaty, Commander Sisko. We will be back."

His image faded away before Sisko could say anything.

"Hail him," Sisko said.

"I'm trying, sir," Kira replied. "He's not acknowledging our hail."

"He wants to believe that we're attacking him," O'Brien said.

"Too bad we aren't," Kira said.

"Actually," Sisko said, still staring at the blank screen, "from his point of view, we have."

Dax whirled her chair. "What do you mean, Benjamin?"

"Look at it, Dax. The station is still intact. So is the Bajoran runabout, which is heading back to Bajor after sending us a satisfied message which I assume was not scrambled."

Kira shook her head. The message had not been scrambled. The Cardassians could have listened in. Despite the chill, sweat ran down the side of her face. Suddenly she regretted her flip remark.

"From the Cardassian point of view, Dax, it looks as if we destroyed their ship."

Kira wiped the sweat off her face. She was shaking. "The Cardassians are experts at revenge, Commander." Her voice sounded calmer than she felt. "They'll come back with their fleet."

"Even when the station is functioning, we're no match for a Cardassian warship," O'Brien said.

Sisko nodded. "I'm well aware of that."

Kira squinted at him. Sisko might know what it meant to be undergunned, but he didn't know how it felt to be under Cardassian attack or Cardassian rule.

It was something she never wanted to experience again.

CHAPTER
24

QUARK WATCHED the medical team hurry through the door. The woman was the young ensign he had been eyeing for days now. She pushed past the stunned gamblers to the center of the floor, followed by a middle-aged Vulcan and a human man twice Bashir's age. They surrounded Nam, who was gurgling. Bashir's hands were covered with Nam's blood. Bashir had worked steadily since the murder attempt, ripping Nam's shirt, binding his wounds, and applying pressure until the team arrived.

Quark wanted them out. All of them. His game was ruined. He didn't even watch as the team worked on Nam. Quark heard the beeping of medical equipment and saw occasional flashes of light. Finally, after a few moments, he pushed his way through the crowd. Most watched in fascination—the human faces pale with disgust, the Romulan faces flushed green.

"Excuse me," Quark hissed at Bashir. "Must you do that here?"

Bashir didn't even look up. He was holding a thin, pencil-like device half the size of a phaser and running it over Nam's wounds. "We are stabilizing him. Give us a moment, Quark, and we'll be out of your way."

A moment was a moment too long. Quark crossed his arms and scanned the players. Rasmussen was picking up the discarded hands and looking at them. Sarlak stood before his chair so that he could watch Bashir work. Etana, the delicate woman who worked as a military operative for the Ktarans, counted the chips at her table. From a distance, Pera the Bajoran watched her. Quark did too, but she took no chips.

Finally, the medical team slid the gurney under Nam and lifted it. The crowd parted so that the team could carry him out of the room with Bashir hovering by his side.

Quark suppressed a sigh as he watched them go.

He needed to get the players' minds off this tragedy. He pulled over the nearest chair and climbed on it. "I think now is an appropriate time for our first break," he said in the cheeriest voice he could muster. "Everyone, please hand your cards to the dealer, take the cloth the dealer gives you, and place it over your chips."

"But it was my first good hand!" the Grabanster trilled.

"Yeah, I was ready to clean up!" Davidovich said.

Quark put up his hands. "Do you think this hand would play the same now that everyone has had a chance to peek at everyone else's cards? We need a break. My brother will make sure you have all the food and drink you need. And remember, we will start again in thirty minutes, whether everyone has returned to his place or not."

He got off the chair and found himself face to face with Rom. "What are you waiting for?" Quark asked. "Get them food."

Rom glanced in the direction they had taken Nam. "But—"

"Later. Go!" Quark pushed Rom to the door. Rom never thought things through. He would have discussed the whole problem in front of all the players. That was all Quark needed. Another setback.

The players moved to the buffet table near the door. Most of the food had been picked through, but there was enough that people found things to eat while they waited for Rom.

Quark glanced at the tables. He had chips to deal with. Bashir's had to be set aside in case the doctor came back. Nam's went into Quark's personal collection. Then he would have to decide what to do with Klar . . . L'sthwan's chips.

Quark pulled out a portable tabulator and sat in Nam's chair. The piles of chips were low. Next time he hired ringers, he would make sure they were good players. Nam hadn't been able to stay ahead with the system flashing on and off so much.

"This is quite an exciting game," said a low, modulated voice behind Quark.

Quark glanced up. Garak, the Cardassian, stood there. "I don't need to hear about it," Quark said.

"Did you think I was going to chastise you for not settling the cheating incident better?" Garak smiled. Quark hated that smile. It looked fake. "I believe it was an interspecies difficulty. Ferengi have a different concept of honor."

"We have honor," Quark said.

"I didn't deny that," Garak said. "It's just your concept of honor is different from other species. I don't believe a Ferengi would ever get killing angry about someone cheating him."

"When Grand Nagus Zind lost his staff to a cheating Romulan spy—" Too late, Quark saw the bait and stopped himself. "Leave me alone, Garak. I have work to do."

"Forgive me," Garak said. "I was merely trying to put your mind at ease."

"My mind will be at ease when I get these chips counted!" Quark said.

Garak bowed slightly and headed across the room. The odor of roast beef stew reached Quark and turned his stomach. Then the vinegary scent of fried banana slug in young Ulian wine covered the horrible stew smell. Rom had acted quickly. The food had arrived.

Quark counted the chips. Less than half the stake. Still it was better than nothing. It would at least pay the monitors in the storage room if the remaining ringer lost everything. Quark slid the chips into a bag.

Quark moved to Klar's chair. Harding sat in the chair next to it, and stared at Quark. "What are you looking at?" Quark asked.

"I was just wondering," Harding said, forming his words around his cheap, unlit Ferengi cigar, "if we will get some of our entry fee back. This is not the quiet professional game that you promised."

"I never promised a quiet game," Quark said. He counted the chips quickly. Klar had been ahead. A shame that such a good player would have to resort to violence when faced with cheating. Obviously he had never heard the expression all's fair in business and poker. Not that it mattered. Klar wouldn't be able to use this money in prison. The extra here would offset Quark's losses nicely.

Quark started to slide Klar's chips into the bag. Harding grabbed Quark's wrist. "Ferengi," Harding said coldly. "You promised us a high stakes game. By retiring these chips, our potential winnings go down."

"Worry about that if you make it to the last hand," Quark said. He had seen Harding play. Quark knew that the human wouldn't make it all the way.

Quark got up and went to the first table, where Odo had sat. At least he wouldn't lose any money here. The Sligiloid scuttled out of Quark's way. Quark looked at the table. B'Etor sat on the far side, only a handful of chips in front of her. Xator had even fewer chips in front of him. The Sligiloid had maybe half his stake. Three of the chairs were empty—Quark remembered when those players left the game—and Etana had the most chips. Her tiny catlike features broke into a smile when she saw Quark staring at the remaining chips.

"Your constable was quite a surprise," she said. "He never played the way anyone expected."

"I can believe that," Quark said. He sank into the chair. Odo had at least an extra fifty bars of gold-pressed latinum in chips on the table in front of his chair. That couldn't be right. The chips were just stacked wrong. They looked like more than they were.

Quark counted. Odo had won. A lot. "This isn't possible," Quark murmured.

"Quite possible," Etana said. "His bluffing style was very unique. And confusing."

"No," Quark said. "You don't understand. He just learned how to play last night."

Xator snorted. "He said the same thing. But no one plays that well after one night's learning. Beginner's luck is a myth."

Quark stared at the chips. Odo had done really well. It was too good to be true. From what the other players were saying, Odo was some sort of genius player. And he's working for me, Quark thought, smiling wildly. Maybe my luck is changing at last. If I can get him to stay in the game.

"What are you smiling about?" Odo's voice came from behind him.

Play it cool, Quark thought. Can't let him think I want him to keep playing. "What are you doing back here? I thought you had a prisoner to contend with."

Odo shrugged. "Once he is in the brig, I have little else to do. Primmon will make sure that L'sthwan is fed. One of my assistants is also watching over him."

"D-Don't you need to be there? I mean, you are such an expert—"

"On what? Helping prisoners pass the time?" Odo put his hands on the back of the chair. "You wanted me in this game, Quark. I believe I should finish it."

Quark's grip on the bag tightened. Can't blow it

now, he thought. "There's really no need, Constable. You have caught the murderer. You've done your job." He did his best to seem sincere.

Odo nodded. "So I thought. Then I met the Meepod in the hallway. She's quite afraid Davidovich will kill her."

"That's nonsense!" Quark said. His nerves were stretched to near breaking.

"And then I met two Romulans who were convinced that the attack on Nam was an accident and that the Klingons were out to systematically murder all the Romulans in the game."

"I've never heard anything so preposterous," Quark said.

"Then Lursa and B'Etor saw me. They said they had some serious concerns about Bajoran terrorists. Seems they are afraid that since the double-cross they pulled on a Bajoran a while back—"

"Enough!" Quark said. He put his free hand over the ear closest to Odo.

"So I was thinking about all of those conversations," Odo said. Quark sighed carefully. Odo continued. "And something you said came back to me. Something Dr. Bashir confirmed."

"Bashir?" Quark wrapped the end of the bag around his hand. The chips felt heavy inside. "We never agree."

"But you did," Odo said. His half-finished face had a serious expression. "You told me poker was a game for cheats and liars. Dr. Bashir said he would be surprised if there was only one murderer in the room. I thought, since I can't help with the station emergency, that the least I can do is keep an eye on the degenerates that you've invited to play this big game."

Quark shook his head. "Really, Constable. There's no need. If there are any problems, you'll be right down the hall . . ." Quark was ready to scream, and his hands were damp with sweat.

"Oh, let him play." Etana leaned forward so that she could take part in the conversation. "He paid his entry fee, didn't he? I will feel much safer with him here."

The others who had been listening all nodded.

Odo glanced at Etana. Quark could swear that Odo's lips were almost turned up in a smile. "She has a point, Quark," Odo said. "My entry fee is paid."

"You can't take more chips out of the game!" Harding yelled from his table.

"Quite frankly, Mr. Quark," Cynthia Jones said from the doorway, "I won't play anymore if I'm going to be continually guarding my life. Mr. Odo will prevent anyone from taking action."

"Yeah," Quark muttered. "Like he did the last time."

Odo frowned. Quark suppressed a smile. Odo had overheard.

"Very few people knew who he was the last time," Sarlak the Vulcan pointed out. "Now that players know a representative of the law is here, they will act accordingly."

"Seems damn logical to me," Harding said.

"It would." Etana smiled at him. "But then, the killer was a friend of yours, wasn't he?"

Harding harrumphed and chomped on his cigar.

"You will stay, won't you, Mr. Odo?" Cynthia Jones

asked. Her gown clung to her body. Quark wished the game was over and he had her alone.

"Well, Quark," Odo said. "It seems I will plague you for the rest of the so-called tournament."

Quark muttered a Ferengi oath under his breath, but loud enough for Odo to hear him. Inside he was cheering and counting his winnings.

And he would win more than money. He would have used his archenemy to turn a hefty profit. Odo would never be able to face him again.

CHAPTER
25

Sisko scratched his cheek. The stubble itched. His fingers were cold. The chill in Ops had seeped into his bones. He glanced around Ops. O'Brien was frowning at his engineering console as if he were trying to avoid the empty main viewing screen. Carter was pale. Dax was still staring at Sisko, her beautiful blue eyes wide with shock. Kira had taken a step backwards. On her face, Sisko could see the memories of years of Cardassian oppression. Her remark about attacking the Cardassians had been unprofessional, but understandable. For decades, they had been her enemy.

If Sisko didn't act quickly, they would be again.

He took a deep breath. "Kira, hail Gul Danar, and continue until you reach him."

"Yes, sir," she said. Her seriousness had returned.

"Having trouble with the tractor beam on the remains of the Cardassian ship," O'Brien said.

"None of the pieces are heading this way," Dax said.

"Doesn't matter," Sisko said. "We don't want that debris in space during this turmoil. Keep trying, Dax." Sisko glanced at the empty viewing screen himself. Its almond shape spoke of its Cardassian origins as clearly as the rest of the station. If the crew at Deep Space Nine had to battle the Cardassian fleet, the crew would have more than one disadvantage. "O'Brien, I want to dig up more about this Romulan technology."

"We encountered it just before I transferred here, sir," O'Brien said. "We were helping out a crippled Romulan vessel when two of our own crew disappeared. We thought they had died in a transporter malfunction, when actually they had slipped out of phase. I think there is a difference, though, sir. They could see us, but we couldn't see them. From the information we have here, the Ghost Riders can't see us at all."

"How did you get them back?" Kira asked. She had moved back to her console. She still appeared subdued, but interested.

"We used an anionic beam." O'Brien ran a hand through his curly hair. "It brought them back into this space."

Sisko felt his heart skip a beat. Could the solution be that simple? "Then perhaps we should be figuring out a way to use an anionic beam on them, Chief."

"I worry about that, Benjamin," Dax said. "An anionic beam might bring the Ghost Riders into our space, but it might bring the *Espiritu* with them. We don't know if those energy creatures can survive here or if we're bringing a worse problem."

Sisko nodded. The last thing they needed were more creatures in the area outside the station, especially with the Cardassians so angry. "Chief, how is Major Litna's ship?"

"Safe in Bajoran space. It should land on Bajor soon," Carter said.

"If the Cardassians return, so will she," Kira said.

Sisko leaned on the operations table. The relief he felt that Captain Litna was out of the way—at least for the moment—was stronger than he expected. He already had to deal with too many factors. Having one go away, at least for the moment, made him feel as if he had lost ten pounds.

"It seems to me, Benjamin," Dax said, "that our problem with the Riders is one of communication."

He glanced at her. She had swiveled her chair so that it faced him. Her words had brought him back into focus. One problem had gone away—for the time being—but the others were still there.

Dax had her hands clasped in her lap. Her knuckles had turned white. "If we can let them know the havoc they're causing in this area, then they may move on."

"They're little more than pirates, Dax." Kira stepped away from the console. "They don't care about the damage they're doing."

"But we do have a bargaining chip if we need it," Sisko said. He stood up. "Chief, you said that they're wanted by the Federation. We could let them know that this area is protected by the Federation, and ask them to leave, letting them know that if they refuse, they will be taken into custody."

"We can't let them go!" Kira said. "They're killing *Espiritu!*"

"We don't know that, Major." And Sisko couldn't add one more problem to his already full plate. He would deal with the *Espiritu* later, once he was certain his station—and the treaty—would survive.

"I think we have a good case for it," Kira said. "When *Espiritu* die, they decay in a way that creates bumps in space. That's how they were discovered in the first place. We have been having a lot of turbulence, Commander. Part of that means *Espiritu* are dying."

"Or," Sisko said, wishing he still had the luxury to be as hotheaded as Kira, "something in that malfunctioning Romulan technology is causing these problems. We shouldn't jump to conclusions, Major."

He walked up the steps to the science console. Dax had pulled a file on the Romulan technology. "Dax, can we send a message to these Riders?"

She shook her head. "I doubt it. In addition to losing your way in real space, the Romulan technology makes communication between in-phase and out-of-phase ships impossible."

"We noticed that on the *Enterprise,* sir," O'Brien said. "They could hear us, but we couldn't hear them. If things are worse here and the Riders can't see us at all, then they can't hear us either."

"But," Sisko said, "the Riders go in and out of phase to hunt the *Espiritu.* They are a group of ships. That assumes that the ships can communicate with each other even when they're not in phase with us."

"What are you saying, Commander?" Kira was

leaning on the communications console, her brow furrowed.

"I'm saying that we might be able to go into their space to communicate with them. Could we do that, O'Brien?"

"It's possible, sir," O'Brien said. "The process of dropping out of phase is fairly simple. I could convert a runabout."

"How long would it take you?" Sisko asked.

"Two, maybe three hours. But there will be problems."

Dax nodded. "In the Romulan experiment the shift was said to be more violent to surrounding real space than the disturbances we're experiencing now."

"It's a risk we'll have to take," Sisko said.

The lights flickered and Dax whirled around to face her board. "Hold on!" she shouted.

Not again. Sisko had loved roller coaster rides as a boy, but this was getting ridiculous. He grabbed onto the science console as the station trembled.

"Power levels in the core rising," O'Brien said. His voice had a tinge of panic.

The lights in Ops went out completely. The emergency lights were not kicking in.

"Power levels at 125 percent of normal."

"Get them down, Mr. O'Brien!" Sisko snapped. Dax had called up the core on her console. Sisko could see the bright red warning light flashing in the near-darkness.

"I'm doing the best I can, sir."

"Power core levels at 150 percent of normal." Even Dax's voice didn't have its usual calmness.

"Chief," Ensign Teppo's tinny voice echoed in Ops. "The core is pulsing. I think it's going to blow—"

"It's not going to blow!" O'Brien snapped.

Sisko bent over the operations table. Red warning lights dotted every patch, but the light around the power core had a countdown.

The lights flickered, then came back on. O'Brien, red-faced and sweating, had his fingers flying over his console.

"Power core fluctuating," Teppo said through the comm link.

"Come on," O'Brien hissed. "Come on."

Sisko bit his lower lip. He hated moments like this. He had enough knowledge of the engineering problem to know the danger, but not enough to help with the repair.

"Got it!" O'Brien said.

"Power at 25 percent of normal," Dax said.

"That's far too low," Kira said.

"Better too low than too high," O'Brien said.

The lights went back out. This time, the darkness was complete. The emergency lighting did not kick in—again.

"Kira," Sisko said. "See what's happening with the backup systems." He debated his next order for a moment. He could have O'Brien concentrate on the power core or he could have O'Brien work on the runabout. The runabout was the better gamble. The quicker they dealt with the Ghost Riders, the safer the station would be. "And O'Brien, we need to get to work on that runabout as—"

"On my way," O'Brien said.

Footsteps echoed on the floor, then there was a thud, followed by a clang.

"Ouch! Of all the—" O'Brien's voice resounded in the darkness.

"You can wait until the lights come back on, Chief," Sisko said.

"Thank you, sir," O'Brien replied.

CHAPTER
26

JAKE RAN BLINDLY down the hall, hoping that the lights would stay on. Occasionally, he would look back. Nog was right behind him, his mouth open and his tongue protruding between his uneven teeth. Jake ran until the stitch in his side grew so bad that he nearly doubled over from lack of oxygen.

He put his hand on a closed door—somehow they had ended up in the living quarters for visitors—and fought to catch his breath. Nog crashed into him, and they sprawled on the carpeted floor. Jake's elbow bashed Nog's chin and they both yelped in pain.

They rolled away from each other and lay in the corridor on their backs, panting. "You think . . . they saw . . . us?" Jake asked. Each word was an effort. He had never been so short of breath. He couldn't remember ever running this hard, this fast, or this far. Not even when he worked out with his dad.

"Even if they did . . ." Nog paused for a long time,

until his breathing slowed. He sat up, resting on his elbow, and massaging his chin with his other hand.

"Even if they did," he said again, this time sounding more like himself, "they wouldn't dare tell anyone. They're cheating. Only my uncle Quark would know, and they can't tell him during the game."

"What about later?" Jake asked. He was finally catching his breath also.

"Later won't matter, especially if my uncle wins." He grinned. "They're probably moving everything right now."

"Why?" Jake sat up. He was a little dizzy. They had run far. He didn't recognize this corridor.

"Because they're probably afraid we'd tell somebody and that person would check." Nog pulled the sensor from his pocket and activated it.

"Maybe we should tell somebody," Jake said.

"Would you look at this?" Nog said, thrusting the sensor in front of Jake. "The secondary signal is still working."

Jake looked at the red trail flashing on the screen. He didn't want to think about cheating and sensors anymore. That last time had been too close. "So?"

"It's close to here." Nog got up. "Come on."

"Nog," Jake said warningly, but Nog didn't stop. With a sigh, Jake got to his feet. It was time to stop all this nonsense. Time to tell his dad.

Nog had disappeared down the corridor. Jake hurried to catch up. He would grab Nog, take the sensor and they would both talk to Jake's dad. His dad would know what to do.

The corridor turned toward a turbolift. Nog had already gone past the lift. He stared at the sensor as he walked and then stopped in front of a door that looked like all the others in the living quarters. The sensor's beep sounded loud in the empty hallway.

"The signals are coming from here," Nog said.

Jake sprinted the rest of the way. When he caught up to Nog, he grabbed the sensor and shut it off. "Nog, you can hear that everywhere."

Then the door slid open. Krax, the Nagus's son, stood in front of them. He was small, even for a Ferengi, but his expression was foreboding. Behind him was a screen hiding the interior. The room smelled faintly of warm electronic equipment.

"What?" Krax snapped.

Jake looked at Nog and Nog looked back. They both knew they were in even deeper trouble than they had been a moment before.

"Sorry," Jake said. "We thought these rooms were empty. We were going to study."

"Study!" Krax looked at Nog, not Jake. "I thought you gave up hu-mon ways, boy!"

Nog's eyes had grown wider. "I have. I was going to teach him the First Rule of Acquisition." Then he snatched the sensor from Jake's hand. "'Once you have their money, you never give it back!'"

He ran down the corridor.

Jake immediately understood what Nog was doing. "Hey!" he shouted. "That's mine!"

Then he took off in a run after Nog. Jake's body wasn't ready for more running, but he pushed it anyway. The last thing he needed were two groups of angry Ferengi after him.

Nog swung up a flight of stairs and Jake followed. They stopped at the top, both out of breath, and stared at the hallway below. No one had come after them.

"They're both cheating!" Nog said.

"Two different sensors. That would really hurt things." Jake wiped his forehead. The corridor was hot. "I can't keep this secret anymore, Nog."

Nog stuck the device in his pocket. "What do you mean?"

Jake bit his lower lip. He hoped he wouldn't lose his friend over this. "I've got to tell my dad what's going on. He needs to know about all this weird equipment. For all I know it might be what's causing all the blackouts."

Nog leaned his head back. He didn't look angry. "You really think we should tell?"

Jake nodded. He liked the fact that Nog had used the word "we." Jake stood up. "I really do," he said. "I think my dad is back in Ops by now. I'm going there. You want to come?"

Nog shook his head. "It's better if I stay away."

Jake sighed. He wished Nog was beside him, but that didn't really matter as long as Nog wasn't angry at him. "Okay. See you later."

He walked down the hall, feeling Nog's gaze on him. He had reached the turbolift when he heard Nog call him.

"Hey, Jake?"

Jake stopped and turned. Nog was standing beside the stairs. "What?"

"You think maybe I should tell my dad too?"

"I think he probably knows," Jake said.

"Not about the Nagus."

Jake didn't really care about Ferengi cheating each other. He just wanted all the equipment shut down. "You're right," Jake said. "He probably doesn't know about the Nagus."

Nog nodded. "Think I should tell him?"

"It's your choice," Jake said. He didn't completely understand the complexities of Ferengi ethics, and he didn't want to give Nog the wrong advice. "I'm going to Ops. I'll see you later."

"Yeah," Nog said. "We'll talk after I see my dad."

CHAPTER
27

THE COMMUNICATIONS CONSOLE had been dead for the last hour. Kira climbed out from underneath it. At least she had the relays working again. The lights on the board told her what the malfunctions were—an improvement from a few minutes ago. But she didn't know how to repair the communications console itself—not really. She had a rudimentary knowledge of most of its parts, but what she needed right now was an expert.

And O'Brien had been in the docking bays for the last two hours. During that time Ensign Teppo had struggled with the power core. Two of O'Brien's other assistants had freed the frozen doors in the living quarters and repaired two turbolifts. Another airlock door was jammed, but this time no one was trapped inside so it wasn't a priority item.

Kira wiped her hair from her face with the back of her hand. At least the environmental controls were working again. The sweat she felt was due to hard work, not great heat.

Even Dax was beginning to look rumpled.

Kira blinked some dirt from her eye and frowned. Jake sat on the steps near the operations table. His dad sat beside him. Clearly Sisko had not made it back to his quarters. He was quickly gaining a full-grown beard. They had been talking in low voices for the past fifteen minutes. Jake had looked flustered when he arrived, but he was beginning to appear calmer.

"Benjamin." Dax spun her chair to face Sisko. A smudge of grime ran down one cheek and deep circles had formed under her eyes. Dax had gone without sleep the longest of all of them. "Five Cardassian warships just dropped out of warp. They have taken an attack formation."

"Five? With no warning?"

Sisko got to his feet and Jake moved to the door of Sisko's office, instinctively knowing to get out of the way. "Kira," Sisko said. "Have you reached Starfleet?"

"No response, sir. And I've been sending out messages since this whole thing began."

"Sir!" Dax said, "I'm picking up a fleet of small ships coming from Bajor. It's Captain Litna, sir— she's coming back."

"Commander," Kira said, checking her board, "all she's got is a bunch of jury-rigged runabouts. They'll never be able to stand up to the Cardassians."

"Just dandy," Sisko said. "Kira, tell Litna to back off. We'll handle this."

"I'll do my best," Kira said, "but I know her. She won't back off."

"Then she's in for a rough ride." Sisko hit his comm badge. "Chief, we need that runabout."

"About fifteen more minutes, sir, and she'll be ready."

"Now, Mr. O'Brien."

"Let me take the runabout, sir," Kira said. "By the time I get to the docking bay it should be ready."

Sisko frowned at her. "You'll have to be diplomatic, Major."

"I can be diplomatic!" Kira snapped.

"Benjamin, I think the Cardassians are waiting for a reaction from us." Dax had put the Cardassian ships on screen. Their presence felt very real. And very dangerous. It made Kira's stomach twist.

"They will get a reaction in a moment, Dax." Sisko took four long steps to Kira's side. His cheeks were hollow and his eyes red-rimmed. The stress was taking a toll on all of them. "Kira, no long speeches about ethics or morality. Tell the Riders that they need to move and that we will not try to catch them nor will we report their presence to Starfleet until it is too late. Will you do that?"

"They're killing the *Espiritu.*"

"If they don't move they may provide the first salvo in a war between the Federation and the Cardassians. We can't afford that, Kira."

His way would save all of their lives. Her way would make things worse. She knew that. "All right," she said. "I'll be diplomatic. But our definitions may differ."

Sisko smiled. "And then again, they may not."

She grinned.

"The Cardassians are hailing us, Benjamin," Dax said.

"On screen," Sisko said. "Go," he whispered to Kira.

She nodded and ran to the turbolift.

Behind her, she heard Gul Danar say, "I warned you, Sisko. You destroyed one of our ships. We do not tolerate such behavior."

"We did not destroy your ship," Sisko said.

Kira hesitated.

"It was you or the Bajorian terrorists. Either way—"

"Give us one hour and I can prove we did not do it."

Gul Danar sneered at Sisko. "You have fifteen minutes." And he cut the connection.

Sisko smacked his hand down hard on the communications. "O'Brien?"

"Yes, sir?" The answer came back quickly.

"I need an opinion. Taking the runabout out of phase in the face of the Cardassians. What effect will that have?"

Kira could almost feel the thickness of the tension as O'Brien hesitated. Then he said, "I don't know for sure, but there may be a directional force to all this. If the movement is toward them it may be worse than what we have been experiencing already. Then again it may not."

"Thanks," Sisko said. "Make sure it will work."

"It will work," O'Brien said.

Kira swallowed heavily. No one mentioned that making the effect worse might harm the station. They all knew it and it was a risk they had to take.

Sisko turned to where Kira stood. "You understand?"

She nodded and got on the lift.

Once she could no longer see Ops, she hit her comm badge. "O'Brien, I'm on my way. I have just left Ops. That runabout has to be ready when I get there."

"Yes, Major," O'Brien said. His voice had a touch of sarcasm. He didn't like her much. But then, he didn't have to. All they had to do was get the job done.

Her heart was pounding in her throat as she got off the turbolift and ran for the service bays. Finally, a chance to do something. Something that would make a difference. She'd take that ship out of phase right in their faces. Then if she got those Riders to respond, the station would cease having problems and the Cardassians would back off. She hoped. She had had enough of them.

O'Brien was in the front section of the runabout. He closed a panel on the controls. "Good timing, Major," he said.

"I hope it's done," she said. She slid into the seat beside him and strapped herself in.

"As done as it's going to be," O'Brien said. He leaned over her and pointed to a new panel on the controls. "Here's our modification. It will shift you in and out of phase at will. Don't do it too often. I wasn't able to test the stress on this baby's hull." He laughed to himself. "For that matter, I will be lucky to hold the power core together."

"I only plan to change phase twice," Kira said. "Once when I leave here, and once when I return."

"O'Brien? Kira?" Sisko's voice came over the intercom. "We're running out of time up here. You ready?"

"It's all ready, sir," O'Brien said. He nodded to Kira. Maybe they didn't get along all the time, but she suddenly felt affection from him—and the affection was what she needed at that moment.

"Good luck, Major," O'Brien said and hurriedly left the runabout. He hit the controls so that the service bay floor rose up to the landing pad.

Kira waited until she heard the door hiss shut before speaking to Sisko. "I'll go out of phase right at them."

"Don't get too close," Sisko said. "They want to shoot first and find out the truth later."

"Standard Cardassian procedure," Kira said.

"Good luck," Sisko said.

"Same to you," she said and dropped the runabout out of docking. All five of the Cardassian ships faced her, sleek gray vessels shaped like clubs. She had fought her entire life for a moment like this and now all she felt like doing was throwing up. She took a deep breath and focused all her years of hatred and her anger at those ships.

With precise motions she swung the nose of the runabout around toward the center of the Cardassian flagship—a Galor-class warship, like the one destroyed a few hours ago—and accelerated.

She waited for a long, long few seconds. Seconds that seemed to stretch into a lifetime as the ship accelerated.

Then she waited another instant, just to be sure.

And in a quick motion she took the runabout out of phase.

The moment seemed almost a letdown. She couldn't see anything, let alone if she had an effect on the Cardassian ships. For all she knew they were at this moment blowing DS9 out of space.

The runabout bumped and shook as if it was being used as a rattle by a giant baby. The environmental controls winked out and the impulse engine light showed extreme stress.

The interior immediately got very cold.

She reduced the thrust on the impulse engines, not taking them off-line because she was afraid to touch too much of the system. Then quickly she forced the environmental controls to start again.

The chill left the air. The hull creaked and the ship rocked. She could see nothing through the port at all.

All she could do was hang on.

As suddenly as it started, the rocking stopped.

She leveled out the runabout and took a deep breath. If only she could have seen the look on Gul Danar's face when she disappeared. If only she—

But that thought evaporated.

Space somehow seemed to be flat and almost had a horizon. Bands of shifting colors rose and then dropped back all around her. One moment red, the next green, then back to reds and purples and then yellow. Over and over.

And every foot of space seemed to be filled with something, yet her sensors showed the space around her to be empty.

Except directly ahead.

What looked at one moment like a tunnel, the next a ball of rippling colors, was directly in her path. Colors on its surface followed the spectrum from red to blue and then back again, then winked like many stars jammed together. The beauty of it made her gasp.

And she knew instantly what it was.

An energy creature.

Espiritu.

And she was accelerating right at it.

She swung the runabout hard to port trying to avoid a collision.

A movement off her bow caught her eye. Five ships suddenly appeared out of the multicolored haze of the weird space. They all looked to be modified versions of renegade supply ships, all marked differently.

As a unit they swept in at the creature.

Ghost Riders!

The *Espiritu* moved away from them—directly into her path.

"No!" she shouted.

All five ships fired.

CHAPTER
28

SISKO PACED as he watched the main viewscreen. The Cardassian warships were in attack formation. Kira's small runabout would be like an annoying fly to them.

O'Brien got off the turbolift and hurried to his station.

Kira turned the runabout toward the Galor-class warship in the middle of the formation and accelerated.

"Their shields are up, Benjamin," Dax said. "Sensors indicate that they are preparing to fire. They think Kira is going to attack them."

"They're not entirely wrong," Sisko said. "Keep our shields up and wait." Come on, Kira. Come on.

O'Brien stared at the screen. "Hit the phase shifter now, Major," he said, as if Kira could hear him. Sisko wished she could. If she didn't time this right, the Cardassians would blow the runabout into tiny pieces.

The runabout disappeared.

"Hold on!" Dax shouted.

The floor tilted wildly, as if the entire station were going to simply tip over.

Sisko fell against the operations table. Its firm side hit the small of his back and knocked the wind out of him. He glanced up and saw Jake clinging to the door of the office, his face pale.

Then the lights went out.

Alarms wailed.

"Life support down all over the station," Carter yelled over the sound. "We have structural problems in the docking arms and we've lost hull integrity in three places, all in cargo areas. No casualties reported so far."

Sisko got to his feet. Damage lights shone all over the operations table. This time it was only the overhead lights that had gone out.

"Power core at 155 percent of normal and climbing." O'Brien's voice was too calm.

"Computers mostly down," Dax said. "All communication gone. Most sensors gone."

"Power core at 160 percent."

"Do something, Mr. O'Brien!" Sisko said.

"Power core at 170 percent of normal," O'Brien said. "I think we're going to lose it, sir."

"We're not going to lose it," Sisko snapped. "Take the damn thing off-line if you have to—"

"Coolant containment field!" O'Brien said. It took Sisko a moment to realize that O'Brien was speaking into the comm link. "Now!"

The station was shaking. No one spoke, but the tension was so thick it felt as if everyone were shouting.

"Containment field activated." Mr. Teppo's voice

was soft through the comm link. "But it's not going to last, sir."

"It'll have to last," O'Brien said.

"Power core stabilized at 170 percent of normal," Dax said. "Looks as if it will hold for the moment."

"A moment is all we need," Sisko said. "Let's get life support and lights back up. Jake, you all right?"

The silence made Sisko's heart leap. The image of his son's unconscious face resting beside his dead mother on the *Saratoga* rose in Sisko's mind.

"I'm okay, Dad."

Sisko let out breath he hadn't realized he was holding. "Stay put, son. Dax, get those sensors up. I need to know what's going on out there."

"Lights," O'Brien said, about half a second before the lights flickered on. Sisko made a quick scan of Ops. Carter had a gash over her right eye. Blood dripped down the side of her face and onto her uniform, but she was at her station. O'Brien seemed fine. Jake was in the same position he had been in, braced against the door of the office. The fear on his face reflected Sisko's of a moment before. "Sit tight, Jake. This will be over soon."

Jake nodded, but his expression didn't change. He was physically all right. Sisko would have to soothe the boy's fractured nerves later.

"Lost containment," Teppo said through the comm link.

"Power core levels dropping." O'Brien frowned at his console for a moment. "Levels now down to 20 percent of normal." He stood up straight and wiped a hand over his face. "I will get it back up to a more regular level shortly, but I'm not sure how much of this up and down it can take, Commander."

Sisko nodded. He wasn't sure how much more any of them could take.

Dax leaned over the console. Her hair had come out of its neat ponytail. "On screen, Benjamin."

Sisko turned to the screen and stood there open-mouthed. The five Cardassian warships floated out of formation like broken toys. There was no sign of Kira's ship.

"Wow! Are they a mess!" O'Brien said.

Kira had done that? All of that? As she shifted out of phase? If the Romulans had realized what their new cloaking device could do, they would have had another weapon.

"Life support back up," O'Brien said. "Teams headed for the hull breaches."

"I hope Kira made it through all right," Sisko said.

"She would have reached the other side before the repercussions hit," Dax said.

The Cardassian ships floated listlessly out there. "Do they have life support?" Sisko asked.

"Yes," Dax said. "Barely. All five seem to be on some kind of emergency system."

"Dax, how soon before we can get in contact with them and offer help?"

"I don't know, Benjamin. Communications was badly damaged before this. Kira's going out of phase has made it worse. It will take some time."

"Imagine if she had been pointed at us," O'Brien said. He was still staring at the screen. "We're dealing with a lot and she was farther away from us than them."

Sisko shuddered. He shot a glance at Jake. Sisko had already seen what the worst was like.

"Sir, I'm getting word from Captain Litna," Dax put in.

"What does the good captain have to say?"

"She says—'I don't know what the hell you're doing, but I like it.'"

"How are her ships holding up?"

"Checking." Dax's hands flew over her board. "They're a little shaken up, but functional. Solitrium waves aren't as hard on Federation power cores."

"Good. Tell her to hold her position, this will all be over soon."

He hoped.

"How long until the Cardassian ships are repaired?" Sisko asked.

Dax shrugged. "I can't get a sense of what systems they still have on-line."

"Let's hope it's not communications," Carter said. "We don't need the rest of their fleet here."

Sisko sighed. "They'll come anyway, Ensign," he said. "As soon as they realize that they've lost communications with their ships. Let's just hope that Kira does her job before that."

"What will happen when she comes back?" she asked.

O'Brien shrugged. "Might not be as bad. Might be worse."

"And there's not a thing we can do about it," Dax said.

O'Brien looked thoughtful. "I'm not so sure about that," he said.

CHAPTER
29

THE ENERGY CREATURE hit her ship at the same time as the shots from the Ghost Riders did.

The runabout flipped and rolled. Pieces of the interior flew with it, too fast for Kira to see. Something sharp hit her in the head. Her straps bit into her chest and waist. She leaned forward, fighting the ache in her skull as she tried to right the ship.

Alarms sounded, faint echoes of the ones on the station. She had heard alarms so much in the last few days they no longer worried her.

Everything was coated in deep reds. The light from the creature had invaded the ship. Kira finally righted the runabout, her hands shaking.

The red faded until before her she saw the white skin of the creature, leached of color and no longer pulsing. All that rippling beauty was gone.

The pain in her head intensified. She had finally seen an *Espiritu* and she had killed it.

She made herself look away.

Warning lights were on all over the control panel. Life support still operated, as well as the environmental controls. But impulse was out and the warp drive looked barely functional. All weapons systems were down and her shields were damaged. A puff of white smoke floated from the console like the wraith of the dead power systems.

Fine, she thought. I show up to confront the Ghost Riders and I'm powerless.

There was nothing she could do.

Except bluff.

She was Bajoran; Bajorans knew how to act when the odds were against them.

The five Ghost Rider ships had fanned out around her. It took her a moment to realize that one of the lights on her control was not a problem, but a hail. She shut down the alarms, then acknowledged.

Her screen came on, showing a middle-aged human man with leathery skin and eyes so dark that they looked black. He had a scar embedded in one cheek. "Federation runabout. Identify yourself."

"This is the Federation ship *Ganges*. I am Major Kira Nerys of the Bajoran Provisional Forces and first officer on space station Deep Space Nine." Kira's voice shook. She could still see the husk of the energy creature floating just beyond one of the ships.

"Lady, what are you doing? You just cost us a lot of money." His voice had a sarcasm that needled her conscience.

Money? She almost snapped at him. That was a life she had accidentally taken. They should chastise her for that. But she remembered her promise to Sisko.

"Killing the *Espiritu* was not my intention, let me assure you."

"Then exactly what is your intention?" He was leaning in a large black chair. Beyond him, she could see a wall covered with charts and maps and rotating computer screens.

She allowed some of the passion she felt into her voice. "Your 'hunt' in this area is destroying ships and endangering our space station."

"So?" the spacer said.

"So?! So I am here to ask you to stop or to move your hunt elsewhere." Idiot. Life meant nothing to him.

"We go where the energy creatures go," he said. "And right now they are all over this area. The wormhole radiation attracts them."

"Your actions may have already caused a war between the Federation and the Cardassians."

The man on the screen shrugged. The motion was fluid and unconscious. His response was obviously not calculated. "We don't spend much time in your space. What happens there is of no concern to us."

"But it is your concern," Kira said. "The Federation will—"

"The Federation has been after us for years and yet here we are. Do we look worried?" He leaned toward the screen. "Tell your people to wait. We will leave the area when the *Espiritu* do."

He laughed, a deep, throaty sound. Other voices from the other ships belonging to people Kira could not see laughed with him. He ended the communication.

Kira pounded her fist on the console. Sisko's communication idea did not work. And she had even been cordial—as cordial as she could be, under the circumstances.

Almost in unison the five ships turned and moved away in a tight formation. Beyond them, Kira could see the faint ripple of blue light. Another *Espiritu,* luring them toward it.

Kira almost followed them, then stopped. She could do nothing. She needed to report back to the station and find a solution there. Maybe Sisko would know how to get rid of these Riders without communication.

She sighed and looked down at the blinking console. At least she still had the warp drive. With the flick of a finger, she prepared the runabout to head back. Then she reached for the phase shifter. Her hand froze above it. The area around it was stained black. The puff of smoke she had seen had come from it.

Kira pressed the phase shifter, but nothing happened. She opened the panel. A small fire had burned in there. Everything was fused together.

There was no going back.

CHAPTER
30

"HE WHAT?" Quark asked. He was standing near the Dabo table. The players were on a five-minute stretch break, and after serving the food, Rom had pulled Quark out of the room.

Rom moved closer to the Dabo girl as if she could provide him protection. She probably could. She was twice his height. "Nog was spying—"

"I know what Nog was doing. I'm more interested in the Nagus."

Rom ducked and put his hands near his ears to protect them. "He is using our system to cheat."

"Not so loud, you fool." Quark made two fists. "Well, I hope it has brought him as much luck as it has brought me."

Rom completely hid behind the Dabo girl. She was moving away from the table, obviously not wanting to get caught between the two brothers.

Quark ignored them. They didn't interest him. What did was that greedy overgrown set of ears who was using his own system to cheat him. Quark leaned against the door and looked into the room. About twenty-six players were left, one of whom was his ringer. He was barely holding on since the systems were crashing so much. But the Nagus seemed to be doing well. Maybe the systems were crashing because the Nagus had piggybacked.

A hand tapped him on the shoulder. Quark turned. Odo stood behind him, his expression grim. Quark rubbed his hands on his pants legs to keep them from wringing. He hoped Odo hadn't overheard.

"I just spoke with Commander Sisko," Odo said. "I have to shut you down."

As if he hadn't been playing. As if he hadn't been reaping benefits from the game. Quark stuck a finger in his ear to clean it out. Perhaps he had heard wrong. "You have to what?"

"Shut you down."

Quark grabbed Odo's arm and pulled him into the bar. Rom saw them and scuttled away. The Dabo girl went to the far side of the table. "Why?" Quark asked. "The trouble is all over. You caught your killer. The game is going on as it should."

"I am not talking about the game," Odo said. "I'm talking about your cheating system."

"Shusshhhh!!!" Quark said, glancing at the door to the back room. No one had been close enough to hear. "How did you know?"

"You forget, Quark. Nothing happens in this station without my knowledge."

Quark frowned. "If you knew about it before, how come you told the commander now?"

"The problems in the station have grown worse," Odo said. "Your equipment is drawing needed energy."

"Nonsense!" Quark spit as he spoke. He had to think. He needed an answer quickly. "It's not doing any harm."

"Ah, but it is," Odo said. "Chief O'Brien believes that your wonderful sophisticated system is adding to the power core fluctuations."

"Well, he's wrong!" Quark said.

"Is he?"

"Yes! We tested them weeks ago. The systems would have interfered then."

Odo shrugged. "I know very little about the engineering aspects of this station. I do know, however, that tests are often different from the real thing. Those little devices of yours have been running for some time now and are making our problems worse. I want the system shut down."

Quark paced around the Dabo table. Murders, blackouts, and now this. His system gone. Not that it was doing him much good. Only the Nagus seemed to benefit. Quark thought as quickly as he could.

He grinned to himself, then turned to face Odo with a stern look on his face. "All right," he said. "I'll shut it down."

"Good." Odo pulled a Ferengi sensor from his pocket. "Because I will be checking."

How did Odo get hold of that? Quark stared at the sensor for a moment. Behind him the Dabo girl let out a small chuckle. She clapped her hand over her mouth. Quark suppressed the urge to chuckle too. He didn't want the others to know that he didn't mind shutting down. Shutting down would improve Odo's chances of walking away with the whole ball.

"You!" he said, pointing at the girl and frowning as best he could under the circumstances. "One more remark like that and you're fired! Now, go get my brother."

"You're being very cooperative, Quark," Odo said, his voice laced with suspicion.

"What else can I do?" Quark growled. "You have my hands tied."

"That has never stopped you before."

"Maybe it hasn't now," Quark said. He scurried away from Odo and went back to the door. It hissed open. The back room was the same: too hot, smelling of overtaxed bodies and Meepod.

Quark looked at the Nagus and smiled. Quark's ringer would lose anyway, system or no system. But the Nagus had been doing well with the cheating system. He had been gathering way too many chips.

Quark wanted to see how well the Nagus would do on his own.

That was the problem of using other people's cheating systems. A person had no control over them when they shut down.

That thought made Quark the happiest he had been all day.

CHAPTER
31

IT HAD TAKEN way too long to repair life support.
O'Brien wiped a grimy hand across his hot forehead.
His uniform felt as if it had been glued on. Someday
he might be allowed to sleep again, but he wasn't sure
when that would be.

He did another quick check to make sure the power
core was still holding steady. Thank God it was. At
least for the moment.

He had gotten life support, lights, and environmental controls working for what seemed like the thou-
sandth time. The replicators were his next chore no
matter what Sisko said. O'Brien had learned on the
Enterprise that when he couldn't sleep, he had to eat.
If he failed to do both, he would collapse.

Ops was bustling with activity. Jake had left Ops to
return to the family quarters and now Sisko seemed
less distracted. He had called extra staff to help with

the repairs, fearing a Cardassian reprisal when they got their ships working again. But communications were still down, so they had no way of knowing if the Cardassians had called for reinforcements.

And to make matters worse, Kira had not reappeared.

That fact had been nagging at O'Brien for the last hour. She should have gone out of phase, negotiated with the Ghost Riders and then come back. Even if the negotiations had been hard, they must have been over by now. Nothing had happened here to indicate that the Riders were still chasing their quarry.

Most of the low conversation was about repairs. Carter was double-checking the weapons instrumentation. Ensign Xiao was reinforcing the shields. Sisko passed O'Brien on the way to the operations table and O'Brien touched his arm.

"I hate to throw a fly into the mix, sir," O'Brien said, "but Kira should have been back by now."

"I've thought of that," Sisko said. "Let's just hope she's having trouble finding the Riders."

He kept going toward Dax. She was bent over the communications console. She had just brought the system back on-line, but whether it worked or not was another matter. O'Brien hadn't had the time to find out.

"Any way to contact the Cardassians yet, Dax?" Sisko asked.

"I had a channel open for a moment, Benjamin," she said, "but then I lost it. I'm sorry."

O'Brien glanced up at the main viewing screen. Two of the Cardassian ships had righted themselves and appeared to have power in the bridge area, although the rest of both ships remained dark. For the moment, they appeared to be concentrating their efforts on stabilizing the other ships. Since the station had been unable to communicate with the Cardassians for nearly three hours, the Cardassians would never believe an offer of assistance that came from Deep Space Nine.

"I have an idea," O'Brien said. "Those Cardassians are going to blame us for this whole mess, especially after Major Kira's little stunt. I don't believe we can talk our way out of this one, sir, no matter what we say."

"I have been worrying about the same thing, Chief," Sisko said. "And I've been hoping that the major gets back before the Cardassians regain control of their ships."

O'Brien hadn't thought of that. Neither had most of the others. He could feel the tension level rising in the room. Everyone suddenly seemed wider awake. "My idea is this, sir," O'Brien said. "The only thing that will convince the Cardassians that we haven't caused all these problems are the Ghost Riders themselves. Given what we know about them, they won't come to our space voluntarily."

"True enough," Sisko said. "Especially since they are wanted by the Federation."

O'Brien grinned. "I can rig a runabout's phasers to release an anionic beam."

"I thought we discussed this before. We can't shoot something we can't see," Sisko said.

"I know, sir," O'Brien said. "But if we can see them, we can shoot them."

Sisko brought his head back as the idea became clear to him. "We need to send someone else out of phase."

222

"Yes, sir," O'Brien said. He pointed up at the screen and the Cardassian ships. "And maybe slow them down again at the same time."

"Benjamin, I have a channel open to the Cardassians." Dax's voice had triumph in it. O'Brien knew what that felt like—to struggle with a recalcitrant system. When it finally worked, the sense of victory was profound.

"Hail them, Lieutenant."

All movement in Ops stopped except for Dax's fingers flying over the console. A few ensigns looked at the screen as if any movement of the Cardassian ships would tell them something. Dax shook her head. "I'm sorry, Benjamin. They're not responding."

"Let me try," Sisko said. He moved to his favorite spot in front of the operations table. "Commander Benjamin Sisko to Gul Danar. Gul Danar? Respond please?"

The ships remained in their position on the screen. Nothing else happened. "Nothing," Dax repeated.

"Have they received the message?" Sisko asked.

"Yes, sir," Carter said. "Their communications systems appear to be working."

"That's not a good sign," O'Brien said. He tugged at his shirt. "The Cardassians prefer silence before battle."

Sisko's shoulders sagged. "Keep hailing them, Dax. We'll talk if they'll let us. In fact, send a repeating message that we would like to negotiate. Mr. O'Brien, it looks as if we're going to have to make those Ghost Riders visible. What will it take?"

"A few minutes to modify the phasers and about an hour to modify another runabout."

"Do it," Sisko said. "And make it quick."

"Yes, sir." O'Brien moved away from the engineering console. "When I'm through, sir, I would like to be the one to pilot the runabout. That way, if there are problems I can deal with them on the other side."

Sisko ran a hand over his growing beard, then shook his head. "Normally I would agree, Mr. O'Brien, but if we're going to send another runabout out of phase, I need your expertise here. I would rather have you keeping that power core intact."

O'Brien knew he was right.

"The Cardassians are going to be watching for any runabout that leaves the station," Dax said.

"Are their weapons systems on-line?" Sisko asked.

"No, sir," Carter replied.

"If they were, sir, we would know it," O'Brien said as he left the console.

"Let me go with Chief O'Brien, Benjamin," Dax said. "That way I can leave the minute the runabout is ready."

"I need you here too, Dax," Sisko said. "You know almost as much about these systems as the chief does. And he's going to need all the help he can get. I'm afraid I'm the logical choice for this mission."

"What about the Cardassians, sir?" O'Brien said.

Sisko grinned. "I'm afraid they'll be knocked around for the second time today."

O'Brien did not grin. If the Cardassians were going to get knocked around, so was the station. On his way to the docking ring, he would stop at the power core and see if he could give Teppo pointers and warning. And just maybe he could come up with something to give the station a little more protection. An idea tickled at the back of his mind.

"An hour seems awfully long, Chief," Sisko said.

O'Brien nodded, getting on the turbolift. "I'll do it in half that. I'll call you when it's time."

"I'll be there, Mr. O'Brien," Sisko said.

CHAPTER
32

"THE FIRST high-stakes poker game I played in was about two hundred and twenty years ago on Titanias Three, just before the plague that wiped out half the population," Berlinghoff Rasmussen said. "I was sitting across from a Klingon"—he nodded toward Lursa—"who claimed to be from the House of Duras, I believe, and if you remember, at that time humans and Klingons weren't all that friendly. So—"

"They won't be friendly now if you don't shut up," Lursa said. She sat across from Odo. She had as many chips as he did, about ten times her original stake. For all his chatter, Rasmussen was doing well. He had the most chips on the table.

The final table. Only eight players remained.

Odo sighed. Not only was the game excruciatingly simple, so were the players. He hadn't had such mindless conversations since the Cardassians left.

"Lursa," Garak said. "Let the boy alone. He's allowed to chatter in his nervousness."

"You see this as nervousness?" Rasmussen asked. He waved a hand over his outrageous pile of chips. "I just thought you might be interested in the story. After all, poker is supposed to be a *friendly* game."

"Who taught you that idiocy?" Lursa asked.

Rasmussen smiled. "It seems your ancestor made the same remark—"

Lursa leaned toward Rasmussen, placing her face only an inch from his. "You have no right to discuss my ancestors."

"Oh, please," Cynthia Jones said. "Fighting at this late stage serves no purpose at all."

She moved an arm and sent off the faint scent of roses. Her perfume was the most pleasant smell in the place. Next to Lursa sat the injured Meepod, whose wounds had festered. She sent off a stink that Odo thought he would never get out of his clothing. Bashir had offered to take care of her, but all she had allowed him to do was sterilize and bandage the wound. That had been the day before, and now, even the bandages were turning green. Since they had been competitors, she wouldn't let him near her.

Odo thought of ordering her out of the game, but suspected the other players wouldn't like that.

Cynthia seemed remarkably calm since she barely had half her original stake remaining. But she seemed to have lost interest in the game and instead found interest in Odo's knee. He had been pushing her hands away for the last half hour, trying to keep an expression of distaste off his face. He had seen her make passes at Bashir earlier, and then when he left, she had turned her attention to Pera, the Bajoran. Now that Pera was gone, Odo had somehow become the most desirable man at the table.

Once the game was over, he would make sure he stayed out of her way.

He had a lot to attend to anyway. Every break he had checked on L'sthwan in the brig to make sure Primmon was doing his job. To say L'sthwan was angry was an understatement. He kept accusing the commander of cheating him. Odo had just shrugged it off.

He was more concerned about what the miscreants who had lost their stakes were doing. Most had returned to ships on the docking ring, awaiting approval from Ops so that they could leave.

But, apparently, Ops was giving no one approval to go into space. And after that last shake-up, Odo understood why.

"Yes, the fighting bores me as well," said Etana, a slight woman with a sphinxlike face. "The game should be the most important thing."

Odo shot her a glance. He had been keeping his eye on her. During one of the breaks, he had checked the computer and discovered her file. It seemed that she had known Lieutenant Will Riker from the *Enterprise* and had gifted him with an odd game, which he brought back to the *Enterprise*. Odo had thought of that maneuver as typical Starfleet inefficiency—if someone brought a foreign game onto the station—a game that had everyone staring into space—Odo would have confiscated it. He probably would have confiscated it upon arrival, assuming it was some sort of weapon, and of course, he would have been right.

The game had been a weapon designed by Ktarans for mind control.

Upon discovering that, he had almost banished Etana from the station, but her file claimed that she was one of the best cardplayers in the quadrant. There were no warrants for her, no technicalities he could catch her on. So he just watched.

The Nagus started to chuckle. Odo gritted his teeth. The sound grated. "Oh, let them fight," the Nagus said. "Then there will be more for the rest of us."

"I think you've shuffled the cards enough," Odo said to the dealer. "Can we get on with the hand?" The quicker this game ended, the quicker he would be out of Quark's. Staying had seemed like a good idea, but he hadn't expected the game to be so easy. One would think that a game with such a long history would have a challenge to it.

She set the deck in front of him. He cut the cards and she stacked them together. Then she dealt, her fingers moving so rapidly that he could barely see them. When both his cards rested in front of him, he picked them up. A four and queen of hearts. A possible heart flush. Quark would have been very excited.

Odo calculated the odds. A heart flush was more likely than a straight flush, of course, but still the odds were not good. He would do as he had done before— put enough in to continue playing, but not raise any bets.

The system had worked well for him, and he had found, at times, that the other players assumed he was bluffing. He had just discovered that if he stayed in the game through at least the fourth down card no matter what his hand (unless he knew he had no chance), his opportunity to win went up. Etana had explained to him, in her own sideways manner, that the players didn't know how to respond to him, so that they altered their betting strategies to cover.

In keeping with his nonstrategy, he checked the first bet and waited for the flop.

The conversation had stopped once the cards were out, as Odo thought it would, except for murmured instruction about betting. If only they could keep cards in front of Rasmussen all the time.

The dealer turned over the flop cards: the eight of hearts, the six of hearts, and the four of diamonds. The heart flush still looked promising.

Garak sighed loudly. Odo glanced over to him. Garak's gaze met his, and he widened his eyes slightly. Interesting that Garak would try to communicate with him. Garak had proven useful in the past—especially against Lursa and B'Etor the last time they were on the station. For a Cardassian, he was a good sort. Garak smiled and shrugged, then folded his cards on the table.

Odd. Very odd.

The Meepod raised the stakes—she was bluffing. All the years he'd spent facing Quark had made him an expert on humanoid liars, and in this game a bluff was a lie. Odo tossed his chips into the center, as did all the remaining players. Leave it to Humanoids to make a game of deception, Odo thought. They were paying to see the sixth card.

The dealer turned over the ace of spades.

The Meepod checked, but Lursa raised the bet. Etana called, and so did Cynthia. Garak had pushed his chair back from the table and was staring at the ceiling, not even interested in the hand. How strange. On the previous hands Garak had followed the cards with intense interest.

Something wasn't right. Odo's cards were excellent. He was one card short of a flush, and number theory told him to call the bet as well, maybe even raise it. Judging from the cards on the table, Lursa could have at best a straight, and at worst, three aces.

Not that it mattered.

Unlike the other players, Odo had no emotional stake in this game. He certainly had no financial stake either. If he lost all the money, it would hurt Quark, not him. Better to get out and watch. Garak had seen something and tried to warn him. He needed to know what that something was.

He folded.

Garak shot him a surprised glance. Lursa glowered. She looked like she would jump across the table and kill him.

So she was up to something.

The Nagus glanced at Odo, frowned at Lursa, and folded as well. Then he motioned to Quark. Quark scurried over, although his manner with the Nagus didn't seem as obsequious as usual. They whispered for a few minutes, then Quark swore quite audibly, and stood back to watch.

During the Nagus's discussion, the remaining players called the bet. The dealer turned over the final card. The seven of hearts.

Odo frowned. If he had stayed in he would have had a heart flush, queen high. A very good hand.

Then Lursa bumped the pot with enough chips to

equal eighty bars of gold-pressed latinum. Odo glanced at Garak, who was still staring into space. Odo had learned much about the interactions involved in this game since the tournament started, and Lursa's action made no sense. No one committed that much money without a sure thing. He glanced at the cards. The seven, eight, and six of hearts. No one bet that much on a straight.

Quark crossed his arms in front of his chest. All the laughter had fled the Nagus's face. Garak was finally leaning forward, but he was not watching the other players. He was watching Quark.

Odo's instinct had been right. Garak had warned him. The Klingons had their own cheating system.

Cynthia Jones folded, and placed her hand on Odo's thigh. He pushed it away absently, too interested in the action to even be annoyed. The Meepod called Lursa's bet, and raised her another twenty bars. Odo had not seen a pot this rich during the entire tournament. Rasmussen called also, and so did Etana. What were they thinking? How many possible combinations of really good hands were there with those cards? Obviously they didn't play using number theory. They played on a system of luck and lies.

How inefficient.

But why should he have expected anything else?

Lursa tossed in the chips to meet the Meepod's bet. Then she raised the bet another fifty bars.

Quark hadn't moved. The Nagus leaned back in his chair and crossed his arms. He and Quark looked like matching short sentry dolls, with identical expressions on their craggy faces.

The Meepod called and raised another fifty. Rasmussen and Etana stayed with the bet.

Lursa tossed in an additional hundred bars.

Odo's throat was dry. For the first time, the game held his attention. He wanted to see what they were doing. He wanted to know what the cheating system was.

All three remaining players called Lursa's bet, but no one raised. The pot was huge. There were too many chips in the center to count. There had to be nearly two thousand bars worth there. All riding on one hand.

One by one, Lursa put her cards on the table. Nine of hearts. Ten of hearts. The six, seven, and eight were already on the table. She had a royal flush, ten high.

Rasmussen turned red and tossed his cards into the pot. Etana set hers down, and so did the Meepod. Lursa pulled the chips toward her with a big grin.

Quark was not grinning. Neither was the Nagus. Garak hadn't moved. He still had his elbows resting on the table, that wide-eyed look on his face.

"I will finish dealing," Quark said, shoving the dealer out of the way. He took a new deck out and opened it in front of the players. Lursa's lips pursed. The Nagus nodded, and Garak leaned back, his body finally relaxed.

At that moment, Odo knew what had happened.

Somehow they had set up the cards. If he had played according to his usual method, he would have lost most of the chips in front of him.

His frown grew deeper. He could not prove that

the cheating system existed, and even if he could, he wasn't sure how he would respond to it. Was it stealing? Could he arrest them? Did he even want to?

He suppressed a small sigh. The rest of the tournament loomed ahead of him, like a death sentence.

CHAPTER
33

Ops was beginning to look almost normal again. One of the ensigns had cleaned up the loose wires near Sisko's office. Equipment that had fallen off-line was back on-line, and nothing had yet knocked it off. Of course that would change when Sisko took the runabout out of phase.

He hoped O'Brien could keep the power core stabilized. O'Brien had spent much of his time near the core with four assistants, trying to find ways to prevent the fluctuations. He had said he was unwilling to boost the low reserves because when Sisko took the runabout out of phase, the boost might cause the core to blow.

It was clear that stopping the Ghost Riders had become the only way to save the station. Both from the Cardassians and the power core.

Sisko bent over the operations table. Systems were

coming up again. One by one the warning lights had blinked off. He scratched the stubble on his face. Too bad he didn't have time for a shave. A shower and change of uniform would be nice too. He was beginning to notice that he hadn't bathed in days.

Odo had just used the comm link to announce that he had shut down Quark's cheating system, and the shutdown had been effective. Sisko had thanked him. They both had doubted that Quark's strange equipment had contributed to the problems, but they didn't want to take any chances.

"We're almost ready for you, sir," O'Brien's voice announced from the service bay.

"On my way," Sisko said. He headed toward the turbolift.

"Benjamin." Dax left Odo's side and took Sisko's arm. "I've been thinking about this and it worries me."

She nodded toward the main screen. The last Cardassian ship had returned to formation. Most still had nothing but their bridge lights on, but that was enough to start an attack.

"I'll disable them for you," Sisko said.

"I think you should stay to talk with them," Dax said.

Sisko looked at her wide blue eyes. In there, he saw the calmness of his old friend. "I'm sorry, old man. I need you here. Once I leave, there won't be much talking anyway. We'll worry about diplomacy if I'm successful."

Dax let go of his arm. She had made her final plea. He could tell from the expression on her face. She knew that he wouldn't change his mind.

Sisko got into the lift. "Just keep this place in one

piece. I'm going to shake them up again. That offense seems to be our best defense."

He hoped. He didn't know if he could live with it if his attempt to go out of phase was the last straw which destroyed the station.

And Jake.

"Good luck," Dax said.

Sisko smiled as the lift lurched and then started down. "Don't you mean good hunting?"

CHAPTER
34

THE MEEPOD tossed her cards on the table, stood and stalked off, leaving a waft of stink behind her. Quark ran the back of his hand across his nose. Never again would he allow Meepod players in his games. At least not without a body suit to keep the smell in.

Quark shook his head. He grabbed the deck of cards and walked over to the side of the room, activating the fan to clear the stench. It was wonderful to have everything up and running again. Just enough to keep the end of the tournament sane.

"Thank all the religious deities in the pantheon," said Berlinghoff Rasmussen. "I doubt my nose will ever be the same."

No one laughed at the remark. Doubtless they all felt that way.

Quark looked at the chips. The largest stacks sat

before the Odo and the Nagus. Clearly Odo did understand poker.

The smell wasn't clearing. Quark didn't think he could stay around it much longer. "Let's take a break," he said.

He opened the door and turned on the fan inside the bar. The fresh air was unfamiliar and quite pleasant.

Quark stood in the door and watched the players move about. They stretched and took snacks off the back table. He didn't know how they could eat with the smell still hanging over the room. But then the Nagus's sense of smell must have faded with age and the others weren't Ferengi. Humans tolerated all types of noxious odors without even noticing them.

The last four players in the tournament were a bit of a surprise. He had expected Rasmussen to make it to the final table. The man was a con artist from way back. Literally. By staying, Garak confirmed his position as the in-station spy. His profession gave him a good poker face. After Quark had changed decks, the two of them had ganged up on Lursa and driven her away from the table in short order. Quark had never seen anyone lose so much money in such a small space of time. He would remember that in dealings with her in the future.

No. The players Quark hadn't expected to last were the Nagus and Odo. The Nagus should have dropped out shortly after Quark shut down the cheating system. In fact, Quark had circled the Nagus's table several times, waiting for the changes. There were none. The Nagus continued to play the same consistent poker he had throughout the tournament.

The real surprise, though, was Odo. All these years

he had lied about not knowing how to gamble. He had to have. There was no other explanation for his stupendous luck.

Unless he was a brilliant natural talent.

He had said the game was simple.

And Odo never lied.

Quark ran a finger along the ridge of his left ear, calming himself. Odo hadn't known how to play two days ago. No one could fake that kind of ignorance.

Quark closed his eyes. Odo was the most natural poker player in the quadrant.

And the perfect ringer.

The odor was finally clearing out of the room. Quark closed the door and came back inside. Rasmussen was finishing off some ForeTee hard cider, his fifth glass in the last hour. The stress was getting to him.

The Nagus and Odo were standing side by side. Quark picked up a glass of cider for himself and eavesdropped.

"You play well," the Nagus said in his tight, nasal voice.

Odo nodded. "So do you."

"We shall see how good soon, won't we?" The Nagus laughed. Odo shrugged.

"That we will," he said.

Suddenly the lights went out. Quark dropped his glass. He heard it clang against the table in the darkness, then cider splashed on his pants. He started to curse when the station rocked so hard he fell into the table. Alarms went off in the Promenade, howling like a wild beast in the next room. Full glasses and chilled grub coated him. His fingers slid into a bowl filled with something hot and rubbery, then little pellets landed on his head. He grabbed one and waved it beneath his nose. Peanuts. He tossed it across the room. He had no idea how humans ate those things.

The station stopped rumbling. Quark stood and grabbed the edge of the tablecloth so that he could wipe the food off his hands and face. The darkness couldn't have come at a better time. He didn't want the Nagus to see him covered in chilled grub worm.

A peanut was caught in Quark's ear. He stuck a finger in after it, and heard the peanut roll around the outer edges, the sound so loud he thought he was going to scream. At the last second, the peanut dropped down his lobe and out.

Quark brushed himself off to make sure no more errant peanuts hid, and then said to Rom, "Lights!"

"I can't find them!" Rom said. His voice sounded far away.

"Must I do everything myself?" Quark asked. He gripped the edge of the table and used it to guide him to the switch. He flicked it and the portable lights Rom had rigged over the table came on.

Rom sat behind the table, a pot of beef stew upside down on his head. Bits of meat and carrot were running down his face like tears. "Get cleaned up," Quark hissed. To look like that in front of the Nagus. Of all things.

Rom pulled the bowl off his head and hurried out of the room, leaving little brown footprints behind him. The Nagus's cackle rose above the alarms. Rasmussen joined him. Garak smiled. Only Odo looked unamused.

Quark pulled a peanut off his sweater and flung it after Rom. This was his own fault for thinking things would get easier. At least this time they had the backup lights. He grabbed a fresh deck and headed toward the table. "Shall we begin again, gentlemen?"

The Nagus grabbed a chilled grub worm off the tablecloth and tossed it in his mouth as he came over. Odo grimaced, and took his chair. The others took their places too, picking up errant chips and putting them back on the huge piles. Every chip from all seventy-seven players sat in front of those four. Quark noticed that a few chips were on the floor and no one had bothered to pick them up. They all knew that at this level of play, a few chips one way or the other would make no difference. The last survivor was going to take it all.

The station trembled again, making the table bounce. Four pairs of hands gripped the tabletop and held it down.

So much for the wonderful extravagant tournament. So much for impressing the quadrant's best poker players. So much for a quiet, peaceful game. But just maybe it would be the biggest haul of his life.

Quark braced himself against the table and began to shuffle.

CHAPTER
35

DAX'S VOICE CRACKLED over the runabout speaker. "Their weapon systems are coming back on-line."

Sisko strapped himself in and quickly checked the new equipment. Then he did a double-check of the phasers. O'Brien had said everything was ready when he ducked out of the ship and headed to Ops to watch over the power core.

The runabout had a dry, mechanical smell, probably caused by all the tools O'Brien had been running. He had managed to finish the task in thirty-one minutes. He must have been working at warp speed.

Sisko moved the runabout off the landing bay and turned it toward the Cardassian warships. They were back in formation and looking more formidable from the small ship than they had on the Ops screens. He raised his shields just as a message came through from the station.

"Prepare yourself, Benjamin," Dax said. "They're arming their photon torpedo bays."

"Thanks, old man," Sisko said.

He dropped the runabout into full impulse while manipulating the phase shifter that O'Brien had installed. Sisko's fingers were moving rapidly and he was breathing hard. The adrenaline in his system seemed to make him move twice as fast as normal.

The runabout headed right toward Gul Danar's Galor-class warship.

"They are starting firing sequence!" Dax shouted.

Then an instant later she shouted, "They fired!" just as he saw a flash as a photon torpedo released from the flagship's bay.

He hit the sequence to shift.

Everything went black.

The controls froze. Sisko pounded on them. Nothing.

Emergency lights snapped on. Impulse was down for a moment, then it came back up without warning. Rippling, multicolored light filled the runabout, dancing across his skin like lights in a Risan dance hall.

He squinted. Space itself looked flat—two dimensional. A white wormlike husk floated to starboard, and off his port bow was the *Ganges*. It too looked like a child's drawing done without the shadow that would give the piece perspective.

He couldn't imagine regularly traveling through this space. It closed in on him, as if he were stuck in a small, tight room with no air.

Kira's runabout looked as listless as the Cardassian ships had after she left normal space. Had she gotten hurt as the ship went out of phase?

He opened communications. "Runabout *Rio*

Grande to the *Ganges*. It's Sisko, Kira, are you all right?"

Her image flashed on his screen. Her face was streaked with sweat and a smudge of dirt ran across her forehead. She had taken off her overcoat, and her T-shirt was also dirt covered and soaked. It looked as if half the controls had been taken apart. She held a laser driver in her left hand. "I'm fine, sir," she said. "But the *Ganges* isn't."

"What happened?" Any number of possible answers drifted through his head: the Ghost Riders attacked her; the runabout was nearly destroyed going in and out of phase; O'Brien's jury-rigging had overloaded a system and knocked the controls off-line.

Kira half laughed. The sound was not a pleasant one. In fact, her entire demeanor was too low-key for Kira. "I had an accident with the *Espiritu,*" she said. "I guess I made out better than it did. All that's left of it is on your starboard bow."

Sisko nodded, just once. He understood now why she was so subdued. She had been angry at the Ghost Riders for killing the energy creatures. Then, when she arrived, she had done the same thing.

"Most of my systems are off-line, sir. Including the control that will get me back."

Another message overrode Kira's and a man's face suddenly shared the screen beside Kira. He had a scar along one cheek and his hair was going gray. Human. "Well, well, well. How sweet. A Starfleet officer coming all this way to save a Bajoran."

Sisko glanced at the sensors showing that five small ships had lined up in a wedge formation behind the runabout.

"She's my first officer," Sisko said as he eased the

runabout toward Kira's. "Let us be and we will return to our own space."

"After, of course, you've dealt with us."

The man seemed too relaxed. Sisko didn't like it. He pulled to the port side of Kira's runabout and turned so that he faced the Ghost Rider's ships.

They didn't look powerful. They looked as if they had been cobbled together from Klingon, Romulan, and Federation parts.

"The major asked you to leave this area," Sisko said. He figured he could bluff them for a moment to buy a little time. "Why haven't you?"

The man laughed. "Really, you Federation warriors are too much. No one has ever been able to catch us. You know nothing about this type of space, Commander. Even if you did, your ship is not equipped to withstand long distances."

The ships hadn't moved from their positions. Sisko could get no readings about their weaponry. In fact, he could get no readings about the ships at all.

"You're destroying a Federation space station," he said, "causing havoc on the planet Bajor and damaging Cardassian warships. Your aggression may lead to war. On behalf of the Federation, the Bajorans, and the Cardassians, I am asking you to leave."

"Commander," Kira said, "we've been through this."

"That we have, little lady," said the Ghost Rider. He was grinning. "And I'll tell your boss what I told you. We can't leave. We haven't bagged our limit yet."

Faint laughter rose behind him, even though Sisko could see no other people. All five ships must have been hooked into the same link.

"Neither have I," Sisko said.

Without waiting for a response, he fired the rigged phaser, hitting the lead ship. Anionic waves surrounded it, making it as white as the dead energy creature.

For a heartbeat nothing happened, then it vanished.

Without missing Sisko fired on the second and third ships before any of them had time to react. They turned white, just as the first ship, and vanished.

The two-dimensional space rippled, like a heat wave Sisko had seen in the Howen desert, and then returned to normal.

The fourth ship turned and began to accelerate. Sisko fired on it. The anionic wave froze it in place, and then it disappeared.

The fifth ship tried to hail him. He ignored the communication and fired. The white light around the ship was nearly blinding. Sisko closed his eyes. When he opened them, that ship too was gone.

The rippling light he had seen when he first arrived reappeared. Shifting from blue to red along the spectrum, then red to blue, wormlike creatures gathered in the empty area where the ships had been.

"Espiritu," Kira said.

"They're beautiful." The lights popped against his eyes. His entire ship shifted colors along with the creatures. He forced himself to look away. "We can't get too close, Kira. We have to go back too."

"I sure wish we could do something for them, sir."

"I think we just did, Kira." Sisko turned his runabout toward hers. "Get ready. You're next. And I warn you: those Riders went back into our space. And the Cardassian fleet was just gearing up when I left. Who knows what we'll find when we return." He didn't mention to her the chance there would be nothing left when they got back.

Kira grabbed her laser driver and shook it at him. "Pretty as the *Espiritu* are, I don't want to stay with them forever. I'm ready when you are."

Sisko fired on the *Ganges*. The little runabout shuddered. The multicolored lights from the energy creatures bounced off the anionic waves, creating a hundred rainbows.

The sight was so stunning that Sisko paused for a moment before recalibrating his own equipment.

Then with a slight wave at the *Espiritu*, he pushed the phase driver and put his runabout back into real space.

CHAPTER
36

ODO STARED at the cards on the table. He had known it would come to this. Garak had lost this hand—and with it, all his chips. That left Odo alone with two Ferengi: the Nagus, who was playing, and Quark, who was the dealer.

Odo would always be plagued by Ferengi. He had decided, sometime in the last five minutes, that it was his lot in life.

He had better make the most of it.

Garak tossed his cards on the table. Odo waited to pull in the chips. It had seemed obvious to him that he had the best hand in that last round. But Garak hadn't thought so, or perhaps he had been bluffing. Someday, Odo would understand the concept of the bluff.

But obviously it wouldn't be this time.

Garak pushed his chair away from the table and stood. He bowed to both the Nagus and to Odo. "It has been a pleasure," Garak said, "and an honor to play with you both. You are both fine poker players."

Odo never trusted a polite Cardassian. He also never argued with one.

"You are a gambler of the first degree," the Nagus said.

"It has been interesting," Odo said "In a tedious sort of way." He stared at the Nagus. Nothing would show up the Ferengi more than to have Odo beat the Nagus. And Odo could do exactly that if he put his mind to it.

For the second time that day, he felt a small spark of interest in the game.

Garak smiled at him. "Perhaps we can have a rematch someday."

"Oh, I doubt it," the Nagus replied as if the comment had been directed at him. "I don't come here as often as I should."

Odo shook his head. "Sorry. I doubt I'll play after today."

"Yes." Garak's smile grew wider. "If you win today, why would you ever need to play again?"

Under his breath, the Nagus said, "He won't win."

Garak didn't notice. He tipped an imaginary hat to Quark. "A fine and interesting game, sir."

Quark's mouth opened, as if shocked that a loser would compliment him. Before he could answer, Garak turned. The door hissed open and Garak disappeared into Quark's.

When the door closed, Quark said, "Would you two like a break? I can get Rom to prepare more food."

Odo shot a glance at the ruined buffet table. Rom had partially cleaned up the food, but enough of it remained to add a perfume to the room. He wasn't sure he could ever look at a roast beef sandwich in the same way again.

The Nagus was evaluating the chips. Odo had maybe only a handful more. Each of them had to spread out their chips to nearby chairs because if they stacked their chips in the normal manner, they wouldn't be able to see each other's faces. Odo refused to think about how much money was before them. He had never really realized how much wealth gamers wasted on these get-rich-quick fantasies.

"I'm fine," he said.

"If he stays, I stay," said the Nagus, and cackled.

Quark brought out a new deck. "Let the game begin," he said.

The Nagus toasted Odo with a glass filled with a greenish liquid. Odo had smelled it and didn't want to taste it. "Now," the Nagus said, "the real fun begins."

Quark sighed, and shuffled.

CHAPTER
37

O'BRIEN HAD BARELY made it back to Ops when Sisko's ship went out of phase.

The wave hit so hard that the station rattled as it shook. Consoles disconnected from the walls and for a moment O'Brien thought the entire station would rock apart. He clung to his panel, never taking his attention from the power core containment. Somehow, some way, it held. He made a few quick adjustments on the dimly lit board. The containment was in place. He really had no idea how, but they were still alive and for the moment that was all that mattered.

The lights, life support, and environmental controls were down. "Dax!" he shouted. "Are you all right?"

She didn't respond. For a moment, he thought of crawling in the dark to where she had been.

Then finally she answered. "I'm not sure, Chief. I think so. Just give me a minute."

The rocking stopped. O'Brien let go of his console

and did another, more thorough check of the power core containment. It was going to need a lot of work, but power levels were holding at 17 percent.

How many more jolts like that one it would hold through was anyone's guess. He hoped he wouldn't have to find out. But if Sisko was successful at bringing back not only the Ghost Riders, but Kira and himself, the station might be rocked to pieces.

In a few moments, the lights came back up and he quickly brought life support and the environmental controls back on-line. A thin haze of smoke filled Ops and the wires that had been down before and repaired were down again. Their hissing, exploding sparks made him uneasy.

"Ensign," he snapped at Ensign Howe who was pulling himself off the floor. "Take care of that mess."

"Yes, sir," Howe said.

Someone got the main viewscreen back on. O'Brien smiled at Dax. She smiled back. She seemed to be okay, considering everything.

"Well," O'Brien said, "I hope someone's negotiating skills are primed and ready."

O'Brien pointed and Dax glanced at the screen. The Cardassian fleet had been blown out of line again. All of the ships were tumbling slowly through space, unable to stop themselves from rolling over and over like so much debris. One ship had broken apart. A large piece of hull glanced off one of the other ships.

"Anyone survive that, Dax?"

"Looks like almost everyone was beamed out of the destroyed ship at the last minute. Gul Danar's ship still has some power and about twice the crew it should have."

"Good," O'Brien said. "The last thing we need now

would be a lot of dead Cardassians. It's going to be tough enough to talk our way out of this."

"They haven't hailed us yet," Dax said.

"If they do you get to do the talking," O'Brien said. "I might slip and tell them that they deserved everything they got."

"Not exactly the best conciliatory tactic."

"That's why I want you to do it." O'Brien returned his attention to the engineering console. Behind him the wires had stopped spitting. All that remained of the smoke was an acrid electric tang. "Life support, environmental controls, sensors, and communications on-line." He glanced around. "We're getting good at this."

"That we are," Dax said. "Now, Chief, we need our shields and weaponry back. If Benjamin's plan works, we'll be hit with a second wave at any moment. If it doesn't, those Cardassians will come back fighting before there is any talking."

"I'm working on it, Lieutenant." O'Brien's hands flew across the console. The last thing he wanted was to be stuck without weapons or shields facing an angry Cardassian fleet. Of course, even with everything working the station wasn't equipped for that kind of warfare.

He glanced up at the screen. When they got hit again, the entire station's systems would probably go down. He wished he had time to cross his fingers. It would sure help if Sisko reappeared smack in the middle of that Cardassian fleet.

The idea that had been crawling at the back of his brain exploded. "Of course!" he shouted.

"You all right?" Dax asked.

O'Brien's fingers flew over the board. "We'll need

some sort of protection when Kira and Sisko come back."

"I will agree to that," Dax said. "But how?"

"I'm bleeding anionic energy into the deflector screens," O'Brien said. "That should shield us from the solitrium waves."

"Shields working," Carter said. "Feeding anionic energy. Now."

On the viewscreen a thin haze surrounded the station. O'Brien nodded and strengthened the flow. This wouldn't stop the destruction, but it would certainly slow it down.

"What's that?" Ensign Carter asked.

O'Brien looked up. A ghostly white ship appeared in the middle of the Cardassian debris. The white faded, leaving a gray hulk. Two other white ships appeared immediately after it, near the same spot.

"Hold on!" Dax said.

"Those are our friends, the Ghost Riders," O'Brien said.

The lights went dark and the station rocked violently as the waves from the ghost ships struck. Then the lights flickered on again with encouraging speed.

"It's working!" O'Brien shouted. "The anionic field is blocking the worst of it. Hang on! I'm diverting all power systems to the shields."

The lights dimmed as their energy flowed into the anionic field.

"Power core containment maintaining," O'Brien read out. "Power holding at 110 percent."

"Tractor beam still functioning," Dax said. "I've locked onto them, pulling them in. They don't seem to have enough power to fight it."

A fourth ship appeared, a bit too close to the station

for comfort. O'Brien waited until the white glow faded from the ship, and the rocking stopped. He did a quick check of the power core to make sure it was stable and then locked a tractor beam on the ship. A fifth ship appeared to the starboard side of the Galor-class warship, sending it tumbling through space.

The anionic energy screen seemed to be holding, keeping the destruction down for the moment.

"How many of those things are there?" O'Brien asked, as he locked on another tractor beam.

A sixth ship appeared at the edge of the Cardassian fleet. The ship glowed so white that it was almost blinding. As the white faded, O'Brien manipulated a tractor beam so that he would capture the sixth ship too.

"Wait!" Odo said. "Isn't that Kira's?"

"Yes. It's the *Ganges!*" Dax said.

O'Brien sighed with relief. He didn't think he could stretch the tractor beams that far. He would have had to release one ship briefly before locking onto the new one.

"The major is aboard," Carter said.

"Where's the commander?" Dax asked.

An alarm sounded. "Screens failing," O'Brien said. "That last hit knocked them hard."

His fingers again flew over the board, but without luck. He couldn't hold the screens or the anionic energy flow.

Kira was hailing the station. O'Brien put her on screen. "You need to pull me in," she said. "I have lost impulse."

O'Brien's gaze met Dax's over the consoles. No Sisko yet. If he lost power in his drives, he wouldn't make it back.

"We have you, Major," O'Brien said. "Did you clean up those Riders?"

"The commander did a brilliant job," Kira said.

"Where is he?" Dax asked.

"I don't know." Kira frowned. "He said he would be right behind me."

There was enough of a pause to cause a frown to form on Dax's normally calm face, then the second runabout appeared next to Gul Danar's warship.

The impact from Sisko's appearance blew the Cardassian flagship end-over-end and scattered what was left of the remaining fleet even more.

"Brace yourselves," Dax said. "We're not protected for this one."

O'Brien held the controls. This time, he would see if he could keep the lights on. The solitrium wave hit the station and made it vibrate. The lights flickered. Life support went out for a moment, and the environmental controls went off-line.

"Power core containment holding."

O'Brien let out a deep sigh of relief.

Kira cursed and disappeared from the screen.

"Weapons off-line," said Carter.

The vibrating stopped. O'Brien brought life support back up, and environmental controls came back on. "What's going on with the major?"

Dax bent over her controls. "Nothing serious. Looks like she got shaken up a bit."

"Did we lose the tractor beams?" Howe asked. He sounded a bit rattled.

"No," O'Brien said. "This one wasn't as bad as some of the others."

"I'm getting something odd on the sensors," Dax said.

"The commander is hailing us," said Carter.

"Open a channel." O'Brien looked up at the screen. Sisko's stubble-covered face filled the eye-shaped portal.

"Quite a mess here," he said.

"You can take most of the credit for that, sir," said O'Brien.

Sisko grinned. "I think you can as well. Seems as if you rode it out just fine. And you have our Rider friends well in tow. You know we'll need to bring in Kira."

"Yes, sir, as soon as we can."

"Give me a full damage report on the station."

"No casualties," Dax said. "Thanks to O'Brien. He rigged up an anionic energy screen that saved us a lot of pounding. Main systems are all on-line. Power core holding. We're doing fine, Benjamin. It's the Cardassians who suffered this time."

"And the Bajorans," O'Brien said. "I just got word from Litna. Her ships were banged around, but no loss of life."

Sisko nodded. "When the Cardassians get their systems back up, they'll be ready to fight. We'll have to be prepared for them. Dax, keep trying to get a message to Starfleet. Tell them we need help at once. And tell Litna to go home and stay there."

"I don't think that will be necessary," Dax said. "Just a moment ago, I got a reading from the sensors. I followed up and discovered that—"

"The cavalry!" O'Brien shouted and the others in Ops cheered. The two Galaxy-class starships showed on his sensors now too.

"The Federation?" Sisko said. "When did we get a message through?"

"I don't know," Dax said. "Maybe some of the messages Kira sent made it. The Federation just wasn't able to confirm."

O'Brien grinned. He worked out the starships' trajectories. "They'll be here, sir, well before the Cardassians get on their feet."

"Good thing," Sisko said. "These negotiations will be difficult, to say the least."

"Maybe we should let Major Kira talk with the Cardassians," O'Brien said with a grin.

Sisko shook his head. "I was thinking instead that she could interrogate the Ghost Riders. I think both sides need to blow off a little steam."

"I hear that," O'Brien said, laughing. Then he noticed just how good laughing felt.

CHAPTER
38

THE SHOWDOWN and final hand came quicker than Odo would have expected. Hours earlier he had watched Lursa bet chips worth hundreds of bars of gold-pressed latinum and wondered how anyone could do that.

Now he knew.

The chips had become a scorecard. The room had blurred into nothing. All that mattered were the cards and the Nagus's time-worn face. The money meant nothing at all. Winning did.

He had to beat the Nagus.

He had to prove to those small-minded Ferengi that their little brains were no match for his.

Even though the game had remained the same, the odds had changed dramatically in the last few hours. As each player left, the chances of getting good cards diminished. The Nagus had taken a few hands because Odo had not bluffed.

Odo hated the fact that the Nagus had figured him out. Odo wondered if he should try bluffing. But that would have him no better than the other liars, and it just wasn't his style.

Quark's communications with the Nagus were curt and almost rude. That relieved Odo. With all the cheating that had gone on in this room since the tournament began, he found himself hard-pressed to trust a Ferengi dealer and a Ferengi player. But he knew that they were no longer cheating. He could tell.

He would show them that their scheming Ferengi minds were no match for his.

Even if he did have to bluff.

The Nagus cut the cards and Quark picked up the deck. He dealt quickly. Odo waited until both his cards hit the table before he picked them up. A jack and eight of spades. A possible straight. A possible flush. A possible straight flush. Definitely a bettable hand. Odo opened the bet with fifty bars of gold-pressed latinum in chips.

The Nagus didn't even blink. His aged face was rigid. Odo doubted if it had changed expression in the last two days.

Except to laugh that awful laugh.

The Nagus called and tossed his chips into the pot. Quark dealt the Flop: nine of spades, nine of diamonds, and ten of spades.

Odo glanced at his cards again. The longer he played and the more exhausted he got, the more cautious he became about checking his cards. In an earlier hand against the Nagus, Odo had forgotten what his hole cards were and had confused them with a set he had had earlier. He had picked up the hole cards just in time to save himself hundreds of bars.

The jack and eight were still there. Combined with the nine and ten, he had a straight flush going. He bet a hundred, feeling odd. He had not been aggressive in betting before. The Nagus looked at him strangely.

"I see you and raise a hundred," said the Nagus. Those were the first words he had spoken in two hands.

Odo didn't reply. He called by throwing in the extra chips.

Quark dealt a six of hearts.

Odo glanced at his cards, not to check this time, but to think. With the cards showing, the possible combinations for the Nagus were a full house or a low straight. If he had anything lower, he would fold. He had done so before.

Odo grabbed a hundred bars worth of chips, a bet the size of his original entry. The Nagus upped him by two hundred. In one quick movement, Odo called the bet. The pile of chips in the center of the table was huge.

Quark dealt the last card. Queen of spades.

A straight flush. An honest straight flush. Odo had actually drawn into a straight flush, queen high. The odds were so high against getting a hand of that caliber that he nearly choked.

Then he realized that it had to happen. Enough hands had been played since the tournament started that the odds—farfetched as they were—had been achieved. It was a matter of simple logic.

He studied his chips until he could control the gleam that he knew was in his eyes. He was going to beat the Ferengi at their own simple-minded game.

Then he opened the betting with five hundred. If the Nagus had nothing, that sum would buy Odo the pot.

But if the Nagus was holding some decent cards, the money would only excite him and get him to bet more.

Provided that the Nagus didn't understand Odo's betting strategy. The Nagus probably knew that Odo had something. But he had no way of knowing how good that something was.

The Nagus called the five hundred and bumped the pot another five hundred. He was holding.

Odo nodded and then just for show glanced at his cards a final time. He pretended to think for the moment, even though he knew exactly what he was going to do.

He pushed the extra five hundred forward. He paused, as if he were considering, and finally, reluctantly, added another thousand.

The Nagus looked up at him and grinned. "This may be," the Nagus said, "the end to a fine game."

He put his tiny hands around his entire stack of remaining chips and pushed them forward.

Quark choked.

The sound pleased Odo. Reactions like that were all that interested him now.

The Nagus couldn't have anything that would beat a straight flush, queen high. Could he?

No, he couldn't.

The odds didn't favor that in any reality and nothing in the last few hours had even implied that the Nagus was cheating.

Odo pushed all his remaining chips forward, even though his stack was higher than the Nagus's. "I call your bet."

Every chip from every player in the tournament now rested between them.

Slowly the Nagus laid down his two hole cards faceup on the table. Full house. Three nines, two queens. A great hand.

But not good enough.

Quark chuckled.

Odo couldn't wait to wipe the smile off Quark's face.

Odo laid his cards faceup on the table. "Straight flush. Queen high."

Quark let out a small hiss of air. Odo watched him out of the corner of his eye. Quark was struggling for control. He doesn't want to lose his temper in front of the Nagus, Odo thought.

Odo felt a small tingle of pleasure. All the hours of boredom had been worth it for the look of horror on Quark's face.

The Nagus stared at the cards for a moment, then nodded and smiled. He pointed at Quark. "You need to hire this man," the Nagus said. "He's the best gambler in the place. And he's local. Think of all the money he could earn for you."

Over the Nagus's head, Quark rolled his eyes at Odo.

The Nagus leaned forward and extended his hand. Odo took it. The Nagus's hand was warm and moist. "Nicely done," the Nagus said. "Well played. If I'm ever in this area again, I'll make sure I set you up for a rematch—with someone else."

He cackled and stood, grabbed his staff, and moved slowly to the door.

Quark was ecstatic. Things had worked out far better than he could have dreamed. Every last bar of latinum in the tournament now belonged to him.

"It seems you owe me some money," Odo said.

Quark smiled a wide and toothsome grin. Odo didn't understand, and Quark was going to love to explain it to him. "Actually," he said, every word dripping with triumph, "you were playing for me. The money is mine."

"No, Quark," Odo said. "We never agreed that I would give you the money if I won."

Quark's heart skipped a beat, then another. "But—but—but—that's what a ringer does!" Quark said desperately.

Odo shrugged. "Funny," he said, "how important the things you leave out of an explanation can sometimes be. We have no agreement. The money is mine."

"You—you cheating, shape-shifting con artist!" Quark said. "I'll—I'll—"

"You'll what?" Odo asked. "Report me to security?"

Quark put his head in his hands. He was jinxed. He was under a curse. A curse in the form of a shape-shifting do-gooder. "Why me?" he whispered to the Ferengi gods. "Why me?"

CHAPTER
39

THE DOOR to the back room was locked. Not even Rom could get in. Quark pushed the last bars of gold-pressed latinum forward. Odo counted them and packed them into the last of the white containers he had brought from his office. Then he stacked the container on the cart.

Quark paced the room trying to figure out a way to keep the money. Odo was right. Quark had no recourse. He couldn't even tell Commander Sisko because Sisko knew of the cheating systems.

Odo stood. "We'll need to unlock the door. Ensign Johnson will be here any moment to help me store these in a safe place."

Idiot constable thought of everything. Quark made himself smile as he unlocked the door. It wasn't fair. None of this was fair.

Ten cases stacked five high. What would a man like

Odo do with that kind of money? Perhaps he hadn't thought it through yet.

"As the Nagus said," Quark began, "it is fortunate someone local won the pot. We need investment in the station itself. Why, just this morning I was talking with—"

"Really, Quark," Odo said. "You know me better than to involve me in your schemes."

"Well, you seemed to enjoy gambling."

Odo shook his head. "The only thing I enjoy is tormenting you." His unfinished face almost eased into a smile. "I think I succeeded this time."

"No," Quark said. "I mean, I'm happy you won. I just wish you would act like a proper ringer and give your earnings to me."

"I never was a proper ringer," Odo said. "Besides, I have other plans for all this."

"You do?" Quark asked.

Odo nodded. A strange expression was pasted on his face. It was almost as if his muscles were struggling for control. "You see, I have no use for money. So I'm going to give it to"—Odo leaned over until his partially completed nose almost rubbed against Quark's—"give it to the Bajoran Children's Fund."

"To charity! No!" Quark screamed. It was the last straw. The very last straw.

Finally the expression on Odo's face resolved itself. Into a smile.

Quark had never seen anything so hideous in his life.

Charity? *Charity?*

He had been wrong all along. Odo did not understand poker. And never would. A true poker player would never give his winnings to charity.

Odo opened the door and pushed the cart through it. He stopped and peered back in. "Cheer up, Quark," he said. "It's only a game."

Quark looked up and watched Odo wheel the gold-pressed latinum through the bar. "Constable," he said, when he knew Odo could no longer hear him. "Money is never a game."

CHAPTER
40

Sisko rubbed his stubble beard. It itched. He couldn't wait to shave it off.

He and Kira looked like refugees from the Zileanian wars. They got on the turbolift together, dirty, tired, and high-spirited, even though they had just left the brig. L'sthwan had threatened to kill Sisko for cheating him, and the Ghost Riders—all five of them—were denouncing him and Kira.

"Well," Sisko said, "L'sthwan said he wanted to join the Ghost Riders someday. But I doubt this was how he planned to do it."

Kira laughed. "I hope they'll all be very happy together."

The lift stopped at Ops. Sisko stepped forward, Kira at his side. It felt good to walk through here, without worrying about breakdowns. After he checked all the systems and talked to the Starfleet captain, he would return to his quarters.

Seems he and Jake needed a little time to work out a few things—and to have that lunch they had missed. But that could wait until after a long, long sleep.

"The Cardassians are limping for home," O'Brien said. "The Bajorans as well."

"That seems to please you, Chief," Sisko said.

"Well, it certainly pleases me!" Kira said before she saw the grin on Sisko's face.

Dax turned from her board. "Captain Higginbotham of the Federation starship *Madison* and Captain Kiser of the starship *Idaho* would like the pleasure of your company for dinner. They said they want to know how you did what you did to the Cardassians."

"Tell them I accept, but only if my Ops crew is invited. You all look like you could use a good meal."

"That we could," O'Brien said.

"Will we have time for a bit of rest first?" Dax asked.

"Rest?" Sisko asked. "Rest? I thought Trills never rested, Dax."

Dax grinned. "Then we constantly surprise you, Benjamin. This Trill needs a nap."

"When you contact the captains about dinner, make certain that it will be at least eight hours from now."

"Sounds wonderful," Dax said.

"Yes." Kira wiped a hand over her face. She only succeeded in smearing the dirt. Her energy levels were still down and Sisko doubted it was from exhaustion.

"Come into my office for a moment, Major," Sisko said. He led the way up the stairs. The diamond-shaped doors to his office slid back. The room was a mess. He hadn't been in here since the troubles began. Shelves everywhere, papers littering the floor. He hadn't realized he kept so many papers.

He shoved debris off his chair and sat. Kira did the same on the chair on the other side of Sisko's desk.

"Killing the energy creature bothers you," he said, not asking a question.

She looked down at her hands. "All my life I've wanted to see one. So I do and I killed it."

"I suspect the death was accidental. Could you have stopped yourself, Major?"

Kira shook her head. "I play it over and over in my mind. I couldn't have changed anything. The creature moved in front of me."

"Well," Sisko said. "Let me tell you something you did change. Before I took the *Rio Grande* to find you, I did some more research on our friends in the brig. It seems that they tried to capture energy creatures alive, but for each creature captured about five died. You were right, Major. Much of the problem we had in the station was not caused by Riders going in and out of phase, but by dead space creatures floating into our space. We had no choice. We had to stop those Riders."

"But you were going to let them go!" Kira said, some of her old fire returning.

Sisko shook his head. "Seems I've been playing poker for the last few days too. No. I wasn't going to let them go. Once the crisis was past, I would have sent you out to hunt them down."

"No offense, Commander, but your bluff didn't work."

"That's the risk in bluffing," Sisko said. "Sometimes you have to show your cards. Sometimes you lose."

Kira smiled. "This time we won."

Sisko nodded. "This time."

EPILOGUE

Out in a now-quiet area of space, an out-of-phase world that the human eye cannot see, a white worm-like creature drifts silently. It twists round and round as if responding to an unseen force, but its body is limp, without signs of life.

The Ghost Riders disappeared and the runabouts vanished, the *Espiritu* float toward their dead companion. They surround it, their iridescent skins brilliant against its whiteness. They nudge it, like children trying to awaken a sleeping companion. When it does not move, they drift into a circle around it and wait. Slowly a hard white shell forms around their now motionless companion.

Hours, maybe days later (the *Espiritu* do not think in units of time), the white creature's shell falls away, revealing a thousand small nodes of brilliant color—sparkling red next to deep blue, pale pink against sea-foam turquoise. The nodes pulsate and grow until they cover the dead creature's body.

Two *Espiritu* from opposite sides of the circle swim toward the middle. They nudge the nodes loose, pushing them like tiny floating balls in a deep, calm ocean. Each *Espiritu* touches a hundred, two hundred, of the brightly shining spheres, then floats away—each in its own direction, trailing the sparkling multi-colored lights behind them.

ABOUT THE AUTHOR

SANDY SCHOFIELD is the pen name for husband and wife writing team Dean Wesley Smith and Kristine Kathryn Rusch. They chose the pseudonym when they realized that their six names would not fit on a book cover. *The Big Game* is their first joint novel, but certainly not their first publishing credential.

Dean has sold over fifty short stories and a novel, *Laying the Music to Rest,* a finalist for the Bram Stoker Award for Best Horror Novel of the Year (the only SF novel to achieve that distinction). Kristine has also sold a number of short stories and eight novels. Four have seen print so far: *The White Mists of Power, Afterimage* (written with Kevin J. Anderson), *Façade,* and *Heart Readers.*

Dean and Kristine collaborated on a publishing company, Pulphouse Publishing, Inc. That joint venture has brought them one World Fantasy award, another nomination, a Hugo nomination, and a house full of books (including numerous copies of *The Best of Pulphouse* from St. Martin's Press). Kristine has stopped editing for Pulphouse and now edits *The Magazine of Fantasy and Science Fiction*. Her work there has thrice nominated her for science fiction's prestigious Hugo award for Best Professional Editor. Dean edits most Pulphouse projects. His editing skills have placed *Pulphouse: A Fiction Magazine* on the Hugo ballot three times.

In 1991 they started to collaborate on fiction. In addition to *The Big Game*, they have sold short stories to *Ghosttide* and *Journeys to the Twilight Zone*. Another Sandy Schofield novel will appear in the *Aliens* series in 1994.

The Extraordinary Novels Based on
the Exciting New Television Series!

STAR TREK

DEEP SPACE NINE®

#1 EMISSARY

#2 THE SIEGE

#3 BLOODLETTER

#4 THE BIG GAME

#5 FALLEN HEROES

#6 BETRAYAL

#7 WARCHILD

And don't miss. . .
ST: DS9 SEASON PREMIERE
THE SEARCH
and

#8 ANTIMATTER
(coming mid-October 1994)

Available from Pocket Books

POCKET BOOKS

946-03

Blast off on new adventures for the younger reader!

A new title every other month!

Pocket Books presents a new young adult series based on the hit television show

STAR TREK
DEEP SPACE NINE®

Young Jake Sisko is looking for friends aboard the space station. He finds Nog, a Ferengi his own age, and together they find a whole lot of trouble!

#1: THE STAR GHOST
#2: STOWAWAYS,
by Brad Strickland

#3: PRISONERS OF PEACE
by John Peel

Available from Minstrel® Books
Published by Pocket Books

TM & ® 1994 Paramount Pictures. All Rights Reserved.

911A-01